What they said about Lonesome Hero in 1974:

In *Lonesome Hero*, Stenson extends the tradition within which he works. Tyrone Lock is a younger brother and worthy successor to Holden Caulfield or Lucky Jim . . . a fully realized, memorable character. —*Journal of Canadian Fiction*

So *Lonesome Hero* joins the list of valuable growing-up books . . . it's a good one, a book that's got that certain sad, weird feeling that you get when you finally get a clear look at the way the world and the people in it work and start wondering what the hell you can do about it. —Eugene Chadbourne, *Calgary Herald*

Stenson's style is punchy like a comedian's one-liners. He's full of frivolous irreverence for everything, but only for a moment, then he accepts. His most rebellious act is to squeeze Revels at the supermarket. . . . Stenson hasn't quite made it as the W. O. Mitchell of the pot generation but he's trying hard.

—George Melnyk, *Edmonton Journal*

Absolutely hilarious . . . the writing is fast-moving, the comedy delightful. —*Winnipeg Free Press*

Like Salinger, Stenson has an understanding of his subject which transcends the autobiographical elements in the book.

—*Vancouver Sun*

Stenson writes with vitality, wit and an original mind; his characters are convincing and attractive. —Kildare Dobbs, *Globe and Mail*

Lonesome Hero is sometimes funny, sometimes sarcastic, and sometimes naïve. Fred Stenson shows real promise as a writer and . . . he's bound to be heard from again. —*Calgary Albertan*

Lonesome Hero

For Monica,
Hope it inspires you
to see this ancient
get a new-old book.

Fred Stenson

All Best!

Library and Archives Canada Cataloguing in Publication
Stenson, Fred, 1951-
Lonesome hero / Fred Stenson.

Originally published: Toronto : Macmillan, 1974.
ISBN 1-897142-03-X

I. Title.

PS8587.T45L6 2005 C813'.54 C2004-907264-1

Cover image: Getty Images

Canada Council for the Arts Conseil des Arts du Canada

Brindle & Glass is pleased to thank the Canada Council for the Arts and the Alberta Foundation for the Arts for their contributions to our publishing program.

Brindle & Glass is committed to protecting the environment and to the responsible use of natural resources. This book is printed on 100% post-consumer recycled and ancient-forest-friendly paper. For more information, please visit www.oldgrowthfree.com.

Brindle & Glass Publishing
www.brindleandglass.com

1 2 3 4 5 08 07 06 05

PRINTED AND BOUND IN CANADA

To my parents, who lived to see this book,
and never quarrelled with me about it.
In their shoes, I think I might have.

To my sisters, Lois and Marie,
and to our neighbour, Joyce McFarland,
who together typed this novel
and got it into the competition
through which it was first published.

But no one really could hear him,
The night so dark and thick and green;
Well, I guess that these heroes must always live there
Where you and I have only been.

"A Bunch of Lonesome Heroes"
Leonard Cohen

LONESOME HERO: The Searing Foreword (as seen on TV)

WE THOUGHT we knew Fred, the fabulously crazy Fred of champagne and supermodels and St Tropez, but here is another side, a shy farmboy with corn-pone dreams and quivering fears, a young Dedalus in the shadow of the mighty Rockies, a portrait of the artist as young clodhopper. No, I hate that tone.

How about this. Years ago this wild book turned the literary world on its ear, a brash beginning novel, a punch in the solar plexus, its narrator a philosopher king bitter before his time, a bad boy, a bit of a jerk really. No, that makes Fred sound like a jerk. Think, think!

Okay. *Lonesome Hero* is a sepia time capsule with sublime fishing scenes, a boy alone with his rod, and by gum, likely much more. Ruminative as Twain, and yet the madly changing point of view, the wild beatnik rhythms, the fake instructional mode, the adolescent grumbling and torment and woe is me, our narrator Tyrone easily offended and offending all, a romp, yet something almost prim and proper about the character, just the right note.

Lonesome Hero rolls and reels, hits a stride, attains a momentum, a blustering comic kinetic force, The Ginger Man striding the high plains. (Now we're cooking!)

Lonesome Hero is funny – funny, and yet oddly touching, affecting as we witness an old-fashioned father grieving his clumsy son's destruction of much of their farm equipment. Or the drunken son insulting all at his parents' party. Disney will be all over this.

Lonesome Hero starts out in rural Alberta – big skies, Chinooks, cases of Pil, though I believe no calves were molested – but Europe also figures hugely in our story. Like the polka music stumbling and drowning in the next goddamn apartment, Europe won't go away, Europe the scowling waiter, the dread destination you can't evade, bloated Europe where your girlfriend dumps you when she finds someone way better. Wasn't Hamlet in Europe? Greek fishing caps are common there, and any number of wars. Crazy nutty place, and it's in this book like a bad penny.

It's like Godot meets Norman Rockwell, *Lonesome Hero* is classic Fred with classic Fred-isms, but from way back, published first in 1974! Before the Giller and Hollywood came calling, before he was given the keys to Metropolis and made poet laureate of Pincher Creek. 1974. Jesus, Fred must have been about twelve, a sonic youth, Thomas Edison was still inventing things, mullets were A-OK, and my uncle Marty could still blow smoke in people's faces on the Greyhound bus.

And now, *Lonesome Hero* is back, for a limited time, if you can catch this slippery devil, he is all yours, pre-punk Stenson in a Stetson, a young man's blues, extra virgin Fred. Run your hands all over him, but be gentle.

I think that last bit can stay.

Mark Jarman
Fredericton, New Brunswick
August 2004

TYRONE LOCK was born on a mixed farm in southern Alberta. On the corner of Rocky Mountains and Rocky Mountains. Twenty-two years ago. To parents who even then were doing their best to work themselves to death.

More notable things happened that year, I have since been told by my father. Two months prior to my birth, he was elected president of the local chapter of the Farmers' Union, something about which he is still quite proud. It was also the year that Murray Iverhorn's eighteen-year-old milk cow had triplets, one of which lived.

My early years were a pampered time. My Irish Grannie competed with my German Omah for my first word of favour. I wish that I could remember more. Recently, I lay on my back in bed, knees up, wiggling my toes, thumb in mouth, trying to pry loose more recollection from that time, wanting at least a bar or two of "When Irish Eyes are Smiling" to come hurtling back.

Sometime in elementary school, I became a misfit. I can point to no exact moment when it began. I grew quiet, so that no one would notice my misfitedness, and the years began to slide silently by.

Puberty was a shock. Beer as well.

After years of sitting silently at the kitchen table or in the corner of the living room couch, I began to stay out late. Once, I threw up in the bathtub and went to bed without cleaning it. I began to scour the library's tiny sections on psychology and sex education in desperate search for an answer to why I prematurely ejaculated in my wet dreams.

When I left for the city and university, the first thing that impressed me was the size of the sex-related sections in the university library. Shortly, I failed all my first round of university exams. I lost fourteen pounds from not being able to buy groceries when I needed them nor cook them when I had them.

An older woman, of twenty-two, began inviting me across the hall for supper. When she took me to her bedroom, I was so nervous I forgot to prematurely ejaculate, and, so, was a success on my first sexual outing. Or so she told me.

The last two years at university were scarred with tragedy. My misfitedness, deked out by the move from the farm, caught up with me. I was driven into hiding, where I ate cheese and crackers and watched kiddies' cartoons. In my more anarchistic moods, I would go to Safeway and loiter by the ice cream freezer. When the coast was clear, I squeezed the Revels.

Now, I am twenty-two and a Bachelor of Arts. Majoring in Economics. I seldom work for money, having some, thanks to being gassed by a pipeline leak in a low spot on our farm.

I am medium height and weight, with blond hair descending to the shoulder. My girlfriend informs me my eyes are green, a surprise in that I always thought they were blue. I have no identifying marks or scars except for the six-inch appendix scar which has elongated alarmingly with age. I mention this should anyone ever wish to identify my lower abdomen.

That, in brief, is me.

1: So You've Decided To Take a Trip

TODAY, I sit in my parents' house surrounded by memories. The Chinook wind smashes against the walls. I cuddle into a corner of the living-room couch. Quite alone. Not quite warm somehow. I try in vain to drown the fearful sounds of the wind with the rustling of pages, the tapping of my toe, and even the adhesive licks I apply to stamp hinges. Any moment, a top-heavy tree could tear from the ground and drop wind-assisted on the roof above me. Crushing me flat as these stamps.

These last days in one's native Canada. Furiously collecting stamps to catch up my collection before I must leave it behind.

I must be off to Europe. The very last thing on earth I want to do. Yet technically, it was my idea. I recall with painful ease the circumstance which began this chain of events. Which will soon cast me, passport in hand, onto an unfriendly, foreign shore. I was sitting with my girlfriend, on giant Roman-like pillows, in the living room of her apartment. She was feeding me grapes in keeping with the setting. I was feeling pampered, safe, and conquering. A disastrous threesome. For effect, I decided to lie a little. To stack favourable impressions on this sweet pamperer. In absolute certainty that Europe held no attraction for my Athena, I said:

"Have you ever thought of travelling? We should just hop on a plane to London. You know. Take in the night life of Europe. Soak up the culture. Slip over to France for the wine and atmosphere of the bistro. Establish ourselves as regulars so as to be let in on all their secrets. Learn languages. Go to bullfights. So that we can be as indignant about them as everyone else is. Swim in the miraculous spring of Lourdes."

So on and on I rambled. Painting a Rabelaisian fresco with bits borrowed from travel agency advertisements. How was I to know she would say, "Splendid," save her money, and send for her passport?

Here I sit, ridden with that painfully self-inflicted remorse. No use to panic. Let the doom seep in around me like a heavy, suffocating sludge. Say little goodbyes to truck, to faithful dog, to ever-spoiling Mother, to splendid stamp collection. Even say farewell to the goddamned wind which may yet kill me before Europe does. Even to the cat who hates me so, I find myself whispering goodbye. I soak up the pain as it bites my feet. Haven't the heart to reprimand.

I refuse to think of Europe. I even wince now as I lick the hinge and press an Italian stamp into a symmetrical row of them. For a cold-sweating moment, I am swept to Venice. I sit petrified in a gondola, clutching frantically at its sides. The gondolier, drunk as a lord and singing "Santa Lucia" off-key, loses his balance and tips us into the oil slick. Buffeted by human wastes and gulping hepatitis germs, I slowly sink. My last glimpse catches Athena grinning widely as she treads sludge. She swims into the arms of the drunken gondolier and I think I can hear her say, "Isn't this glorious, Tyrone?" The bloated body of a cat floats by.

I haven't the slightest interest in museums, tire easily of historical buildings, and would just as soon not learn how the other half or nine-tenths live. So, why, oh why, go to Europe? Being trampled and elbowed and eye-gouged by vacant-eyed tourists as I stand a hundred feet of solid people away from a bobbing row of furry black hats that I'm only taking somebody's word for being atop the Queen's guards' heads. The holidaying horde shooting films of them with revolver movie cameras held at arm's length to get above the crowd, only to find that their aim was bad and all they've got to show the folks at home of the marching guards are underexposed five-minute features of the second-storey windows of Buckingham Palace.

But it won't be the Europeans' fault if I am killed. Maimed in a busy street, a little car atop my chest. They didn't ask me to come. I did it all by myself. Invited myself to miserable, unfriendly death on foreign soil by a so-thought harmless boast of adventurousness. Is this what adventurous means? To place one's body on a rack of foreign torture? To stuff one's cherished digestive system with weird foods which it does not know how to process?

Out into the gale, I think. I will stand downwind of the trees. A branch will rip off. About the size of my arm and strike me down. Into the hospital I will go, unless dead. To lie in antiseptic, domestically made sheets safely unable to travel possibly for years. Blood thumps in my brain. I can stamp-collect no longer. Too remindful of prospective death-trip abroad. I'll cuddle here in comfy couch corner. So absolutely at home. Now I'll snap on the TV and get lost for two hours in the escapades of a western movie hero.

"For this week only, Wild West Night at the Movies has been cancelled so that we can bring you a special report on the progress to date of Britain's entry into the European Economic Community."

Snap. The room goes dark and I watch the bead of light in the centre of the screen until it too dies. There is darkness everywhere as my life breaks into ever smaller pieces. Torn from my orbit, I will wander forever lost.

2: Purchasing Necessary Supplies

TYRONE LOCK in a sporting goods store. Dressed more warmly in woollen cardigan and gloves than the weather warrants. What the observer cannot see is that he has the winter liner zipped into his trench coat as well. He walks slowly from truck to store so as not to sweat. Now facing ruddy-faced sportsman who grins with health.

"Can I help you there, Doc?" Sportsman leans over Arborite, several teeth showing for his sales pitch. Views Tyrone as a sucker easily caught up in the race to have the latest equipment.

"You must be hot in all those clothes, Doc. It's a beautiful day out."

"No."

"No what?"

"No on both counts."

"Oh, well what can I do for you, Doc?"

"I want a backpack."

"Oh, a pack. Yeah, well we got all the latest in packs. Now this. You'll like this. It has an automatic flotation balloon built right into it. If you fall in a lake, you just pull this little handle and bingo! instant life jacket. A little expensive some might say. But when you think of all the advantages, it's probably cheaper value-wise than a lot of these others."

"I don't hike near lakes or rivers. What I want is one that is light and cheap."

"You're a long-distance hiker, are you?"

"Short distance."

"Oh, well we have this one here with . . ."

"How much?"

"Here on the label, Doc."

"Too much."

"This one then."

"Also too much. I want one for twenty dollars."

"We only have one that's that cheap."

"I'll take it."

"It'll fall apart on you, Doc."

"Good. Then I'll stop hiking."

A good-humoured ring of the register. Money transferred. Twenty dollars in and a penny back. Tyrone slips it in a special pocket of his trench coat marked "S" for stingy.

TYRONE LOCK in a drugstore. A lady behind the counter dressed in flashing white smiles up at him. She always feels happy selling goodies to make the sick well. She feels not only good but holy.

"Good afternoon, sir. What can I do for you? Have you a fever that you're wearing so much?"

"No on both counts."

"Wasn't that just one, sir?"

"It's not a beautiful day either and that makes two."

"You poor dear. You're not well, are you?"

"Yes on one count. I am fine. I have a list of the ten most prominent sicknesses in Europe. I want a guaranteed prevention or cure for all of them."

"Oh dear." Little lady takes the slip. She is dazed. Thinking this has never happened before. "I don't know, sir. I only fill prescriptions. You would have to go to a doctor."

"He would only send me back here. Fill the prescription."

"Now sir, this is not a prescription."

"It is."

"Doctors issue prescriptions. You wrote this list yourself."

"A prescription is an order for drugs. This list combined with my instructions is also an order for drugs. Therefore, this is a prescription. Now fill it."

"This is not a prescription."

"You, madam, are incompetent."

"I'm calling the police."

"I was just leaving."

"In thirty years, I have never had a complaint. Everyone has always complimented me on my devotion to my work."

The lady in white begins to cry, and Tyrone leaves, little list in hand.

3: Choosing a Travelling Companion

THE SUN will soon go down on another Canadian day. So few left before takeoff and exile. Already the sky above the Rockies is a candy-floss pink. Paying tribute to raging forest fires somewhere below.

Matches the redness of my farm truck which bears me at madcap pace between hills. I am eager to be snuggled in front of my parents' TV. I wouldn't pick my nose if I wasn't so nervous. Quite a trick really, as it requires that I raise one hand from the wheel. Could lower my head to my waiting finger. But no, that would be even more daring.

Now I am smoking. Suspending my nose-picking for the moment. Any way that I can soothe my nerves will do. One of the many reasons why I must smoke. If I quit, I would find myself in restaurants reaching for the nose to answer the inner need. Or merrily picking over my beer in the tavern. People moving disgustedly away. Athena of course would leave me. Suffering to think that she'd ever given her love to a pick-nose.

Looking at it analytically, what is really wrong with picking one's nose? Not any more disgusting than scratching at dandruff. Society has inhibitions as regards any orifice, I suppose. It's a lewd-thinking society that condemns us.

I sit here picking languidly again. Driving very slowly now. All the big hurry gone as I contemplate a utopia where a pick-nose could aspire to public office. And all institutionalized cowards would be granted amnesty.

SOON HOME and in front of our lovely television set. With its graceful lines. And many-coloured knobs. It lights up the dark room with fast-moving shadows. Flickering across me. Giving me a ghostly pallor, no doubt.

Such a better way to travel. To board the magic tube and sail to anywhere on celluloid tracks. And never leave the comfort of my couch.

My father walks in. Tired from a long day of riding his grunting tractor. He stands near by. Apparently wishing to start a conversation.

"What's on?"

"Living colour."

"What in living colour?"

"An exposé of life."

Father remains. Pretending to watch. This exposé of life.

"How's Athena?"

"I will be available for comment at the next commercial break."

Father persists.

"I hear you're going to Europe."

I roll over onto my back and stare through light beams at the ceiling. Thinking, so that's why.

"Yes, I'm going to Europe."

"Go ahead and watch your program if you like."

"No, its all right. It was a fairly poor exposé of life anyway."

"Where are you going exactly? Or do you know?"

"Across a wide sea."

"I know where it is. You don't seem very pleased about it."

"I'm pleased. See, I'm smiling."

"Yeah."

"Did you plough a field today?"

"Yeah, I'm doing the summer fallow on the far east quarter again."

"That's nice." I pick up my guitar and strum a minor chord string by string, very slowly. My mind sings a single lyric. Doom. Doom. Doom. My father leaves, closing the kitchen door, to sit across from my mother and whisper, "I think we did something wrong with that boy."

I strum on. D minor. D minor. D minor. I sing Doom, Doom and then say etc. and know what I mean anyway.

Suddenly another voice in the kitchen. Athena! I know it is she. Has come to see me over miles and miles. I rate. So nice to rate with one so pretty. She is talking to my father. They are fond of one another. Athena, being more sane than I, puts hope in my father's autumn days. Hope for pretty grandkiddies. Patter of little feet again on the old kitchen floor. Bring out the toy box from its dusty cupboard. I get up and walk to the kitchen.

"Hi, sweetie." We have a little hug. "Were you watching that thing again? It's going to rot your eyes, Ty."

"I was strumming the other thing."

"Oh yeah? You haven't played in a long while. Were you learning that song I've been begging you to learn?"

"No, I was writing one."

"Oh far out! Have you named it yet?"

"Yes. It's called 'Doom.'"

"Oh. Well let's go. I want to hear it."

"No. I'm not completely satisfied with it yet."

Grinning wide, she chucks me under the chin and addressing my father says, "He's such a perfectionist, he never gets anything quite ready." Then to me, "You know, I've never heard you sing a note."

"My heart sings constantly, but no one listens."

"Oh, poor baby." We link arms and into the living room we go. The TV buzzes on. A new world has commenced on the sacred tube. The dimly lit room full of these new shadows. Ours mingling in. Quite a concept really. That this man on the TV, whether he is in Siam or dead, has his shadow, at this moment, in my house. I wonder what Descartes would make of that.

We sit and are now so closely pressed.

"Aren't you going to ask me why I'm here?"

"I presume you've come to see me."

"Of course I've come to see you. You're always fishing for those little words, aren't you? You know what I mean."

"You mean, I suppose, what set of circumstances enabled you to come on this twilight ride to my old country home on a night when you'd ordinarily be going to bed early to prepare yourself for an early morning of wrapping the limbs of chickens in pieces of cellophane."

"Yeah, that's about it, Tyrone."

"Well, what set of circumstances did enable you to come on a night . . ."

"I quit, Tyrone. No more chickens!"

"Then you aren't going to Europe after all?" Suppress that note of hope in the voice. Keep those syllables monotone.

"Of course I'm going. I landed another job, that's all. No more chickens. I'm going to be a classy secretary for better money starting this coming week. I told my chicken-stuffing boss to pack the three million chicken legs I've wrapped there right up himself! Crossways! Oops! Did I say that loudly? I keep forgetting that your parents think I'm sort of an untouched lily of the valley. I really like your folks, Tyrone. I mean, they're so quaint."

"Rustic too."

"I'm sorry. I wasn't trying to be offensive."

"Go ahead. The wounds will heal."

"Anyway, I got this new job and I make a half more per hour and I don't start till Monday. Therefore, here I am in the home of Mr. Tyrone Lock. My own personal sweetie pie."

"I'm glad, Athena. You never did smell good in chickens."

"Let's neck, Tyrone. All over the couch. Just like little high-school kids. Scared to death that your folks might come in."

"That doesn't seem so old-fashioned to me. High school wasn't that long ago. At twenty-two I am still a veritable lad."

"You act like you're a hundred sometimes."

"It's my wisdom backing up like a sewer."

"You know, I wonder about you sometimes, Tyrone."

"Some day, Athena, all will wonder at me, rather than about me."

"Sure I can read it now. In all the papers: 'Tyrone Lock, Wonder of the Age, discovers the cure for cancer.'"

"Do you want my autograph now? Or after I become famous?"

"I can do even better than that." Ooh, what a nice, nasty grin I see there. "Come here, Tyrone."

Athena's weight pressing me down on this couch. So victimized and so nice to be. Trapped by this mound of womanhood. So hungry for little me.

"Tyrone, you little devil. Huffing and grunting like that. You should hear yourself. You sound just like a little bull."

"That could be because I'm suffocating."

"That's not very romantic. I like it better my way. I like it when you're like a little bull."

"Moo."

"Let's go for a drive in your truck. We'll say that I've always wanted to see the feedlot in the dark or that I've never seen a cow sleep standing up."

"Moo."

Into the darkness, the edges of my headlights' beams like the walls of a cave. The moon peeping out in flashes as the clouds drift by. And I inscribe curves on this little piece of world.

I stop at the old baseball diamond. And say it's so that I can get to first base with her. Athena laughs and we go to bat in the top half of the first inning. Looks as if I am going to get an intentional walk.

A friend once said that he thought about soccer. Said it made him last longer. I would just as soon keep soccer and sex on different plateaus. The baseball game continues. Later I may move to second base and third. Strictly amateur stuff here. We wear no spikes, so as not to cause hurt while sliding. And seldom hit grand slams or steal bases. Athena cuddling close, shivering. Says she's always been afraid of situations like this. That she might look up to find me covered in hair, a row of yellow fangs hanging out of my furry face. Says she's even afraid to look now. Woof. Woof. I say. She says she heard once that a couple had a flat tire by a graveyard. No spare. The fellow had gone out to get assistance. He'd said lock the doors and let in no one. He never returned. She sat there cold and terrified. There was a constant scratching on the roof. She thought it was a tree branch. The police found her the next morning still locked inside the car. Her boyfriend's severed head on top of the roof. Ha. Ha. I say. How ridiculous, I say.

I hear noises. I will go out to take a wee-wee. My severed head will be found on the top of my cab – a baseball cap atop it. Skull and crossbones where the team emblem should be. Athena would put a little drop of my blood in a vial and look at it once in a while. A strange mixture of feelings running through her. I hope gladness would not be one of them. Perhaps it would be if Mr. More Right comes along after my tragic demise. How selfish to think that if I died, I would wish to be irreplaceable. To wish Athena to always pine the loss of me. I find a perverse peace in such a thought. To have her staring at my picture and perusing my stamps each day she lived after I was gone. To have her become a nun for the worship of only me.

It always seems that afterward, a mystical conversation should ensue. On some weird subject not yet invented. Some day, Filial Cosmography or Post-Universal Antiquarianism, or something else which presently means nothing, may be a tradition in post-coital chat. Something so mystical and revered that it will demand its own private alphabet. The symbols joining through a natural power embodied in themselves, to form words with an idea-power, again all of their own. Which will, of course, change all concepts. It will be linked only with one contemporary idea, that of sex. The only action which approaches the mythology of this self-created creation. A totally new way of looking at Holy Communion. I can hardly wait.

"Tyrone, why don't you ever help your father around the farm?" Another beautiful image lies broken.

"I am very busy, Athena. I have explained that to my father, but he doesn't understand. I've tried."

"Bullshit, Tyrone. All you're doing is watching TV and taking weird trips in your truck. Excuse me, and playing your guitar and collecting stamps."

"I'm preparing myself mentally." Please Athena, I say to myself, do not make me say what for.

"What in hell for, the afterlife?"

Athena should listen to her subconscious. It betrays its knowledge of the future.

"For the trip."

"Well, that might explain the weird trips you've been taking; but otherwise, it's a mystery. I don't blame your father for not understanding."

"I'm preparing myself mentally. I think that's important."

"You're weird, Tyrone. I often wonder why I dig you so much."

"I have a very poetic soul. Besides, just last week, I went out and chopped down a wheat field."

"Yeah, and I know exactly what happened too. Your father told me. The reel jammed up with green grain and you didn't notice for a round and a half. By that time, the entire machine was wrecked. Whatever the lathes are, they were all broken. And so was the clutch slip."

"Slip clutch." I correct out of memory rather than knowledge.

"Well, anyway, your father said the machine needed a major overhaul by the time you were finished with it. He actually had to hire someone to finish the field. He says you hardly know which end of the tractor is the front."

"Not entirely true. Unless climate or the character of the machine intervenes, I can turn it off or on. My knowledge of the other buttons and dials increases with every outing."

"Which are seldom. It's just that your parents are such sweet people. You never try to help them out and you're always being weird with them. I really think they think you're crazy."

"An easy thing to think, but not an easy thing to be."

"Don't get weird with me too, Tyrone. I don't like it. It always makes me feel like you're trying to lock me out." Athena, I think, you strike so close.

"You're sort of like a big vault and I'm sort of like a safecracker. You see, Tyrone, I have this feeling you could be perfect for me. I'm not talking about marriage, so don't get scared. What I mean is that you just sort of slip me crumbs of what you're like, out under the door, and I'm crazy about those crumbs. They're what I really crave about you. And I'm greedy. I want to break in and get at everything. Am I making sense?"

I will not say how much, but I will say, "Athena, did it ever occur to you that the crumbs might be good because the loaves of bad things are too big to leak out?"

"Tyrone, you're sweet. I'll never believe that."

And you'll never know it's true. I look at her sun-baked brownness and the sweet lines of that head in which so many truths amble aimlessly. I will dare foreign soil to be with one so nicely fitted. For she will take care of my mortal remains. In this only do I trust.

THE ROCKY Mountains make a slow curve from northwest to due south in the southwest of Alberta. They rise abruptly from the foothills, and where they run along the Canada–United States border they end just as abruptly in a mountain surnamed Chief. In their southwest hinge lies a national park named Waterton and where the Waterton townsite meets the lake edge, two people lie stretched on a blanket.

"It's so pretty here, Tyrone. The way the water bounds up at us and then goes back."

"I was reading you a beautiful poem and you interrupted."

"What's so great about a couple having oral sex?"

"I think he's sitting in a chair."

"Ugh! That's worse." There's a pause full of the sound of waves flopping. "Does that really appeal to you, Tyrone?"

"He makes it mystical, Athena. Aren't you getting that?"

"Tyrone, you've read it six times and the only vision I've got from it is a reprint from a Scandinavian skin magazine a guy gave me one time."

"I don't want to hear about your past, Athena."

"That limits me, Tyrone. You could wind up hearing a lot about the weather."

"You know what I mean."

"Yes, I do. I was only being a little obstinate. The woman's prerogative: five seconds of liberation per day. Besides the guy was a shithead. Most people who subscribe to Sweden for porno are."

"I feel like this poet is really touching on something."

"I should hope so." Tyrone stares. "Sorry. Forget I uttered."

"He's getting the idea of sex as something which transcends both the physical and the spiritual."

"What's left?"

"Everything, Athena. I really think that. That for everything there is, for each level of existence and non-existence, there is a higher level where the first non-existence is the existence. I'm saying that the that-which-no-greater-can-be-conceived-of exists only for that which is lesser than it."

Tyrone smiles self-appreciatingly.

"Tyrone, doesn't it get lonely up there?"

"Up where?"

"Well, maybe it's down there, no offence."

"Down where?"

"Where all those weird ideas get created. I mean, there you are saying something to me which you must know is meaningless to me. I mean, maybe the idea in your mind that the words come from seems sane to you, but I can't make head nor tail of it and I don't think a person living, except you, could. I just think it must get lonely in there with all those private inklings."

"The private inklings of Descartes fill many books."

But he knows that she is right; that she has again walked in to poke a hole in his world made of such pierceable things. She has cleverly steered her ship very close to his camouflaged harbour once again. How long will it be before she lobs a bomb? Or will she discover only to surrender?

4: How To Make Best Use of Your Luggage Space

WALKING ALONG on this so-calm day. Fine-spun cloud drifting lazily in this pale blue autumn sky. Just a bit of breeze to lift my hair and gently replace it. On this Monday morning, I have said goodbye to Athena. She hopped in behind the wheel of her little car as the sun peeped up, to speed along with great daring into the fiery red horizon. To Brookside, her small home city, one hundred flat, straight miles to the east. To arrive a minute early behind her shiny new desk. To be jaunty at her work. To type at great speed and set her boss's old heart aflutter. As she takes down a letter in a pad atop her crossed legs. The rustling of her nylons when she moves causing him to take a pill to tranquilize his hammering heart. Fine as long as he keeps both hands fixed to market reports.

And I, a breakfast and two yawning hours after the farewell, now walk the fields to check the cattle. A task my father trusts me with. I look at their feet for swelling; scare them onto their feet when I think they might limp. I count them – my father knows that I count quite well and am capable of matching my total with the number he tells me there should be. I know symptoms for a few of the diseases that plague them. I listen for their coughing and check their udders for too much milk. I watch the calves for any that might look gaunt or seedy with lice. I have been known to come within a matter of days in the guessing of a cow's maternal moment, to the amazement of my father who thinks I am incapable of anything but the easiest association task.

Do I sound sarcastic? I mean to, but not in cruelty. I know I am not a son farm-fathers dream of. I know I do things that put my sanity in doubt. I blame no one. Certainly not myself. There is of course an excuse, but it balks at verbalization. Another of what Athena calls my "private inklings." At least I don't wallow in the common generalization. I think it is a bit commendable that I don't say, "Who in reality can explain himself?" or "Why does anyone do what he does?"

But enough! I walk now in great peace. Under a secure and friendly sky. The grass making dewy squishes under each foot. Up, old cow, I say. Hold your cud and promenade a moment for me. The way you stare from those brown orbs as if you'd never seen an item on two feet before. Retain that innocence, old deary. And pray, in your spare moments between breeding, eating, and giving birth, that your babes will be strong and healthy so you are granted the privilege of death in the pasture by natural causes. I wish that you may die after a hardy eighteen years and without ever knowing the maddening tingle of a stock-prod in your arse.

So satisfied would I be to languish here; all my talents and capacities going to total waste. Athena at my side, cursing vociferously when she steps in fresh dung. Ruining another pair of brand new suedes.

I look across these brown hills and my life becomes compressed to a moment. I see the school I went to when I was six, the route by which my bus bore me home from the town school that came later, the stormy sky in the mountain nook where Waterton lies lonely after another tourist season; the various gullies and river bottoms where I drank my first bottles of beer, tossed my first beery biscuits, and grappled with girls for the privilege of putting my hands in places where they ached to go.

My life stands summarized.

How sad that my short future will be spread like bird droppings. In small dots across foreign places. It will lie broken and forgotten. Less than forgotten; never known. A nostalgia rushes through me in choking intensity. Suddenly, I am whistling "O Canada." I feel silly but do not stop. Wish only that there was a more regional tune to whistle or sing.

O Beaver Creek,
In the Foothills of Alberta's Rocky Mountains,
I would sooner have you,
Than a bunch of crappy marble fountains.

THE TINNY backpack sits in the corner, an unwanted addition to my room. Its empty sack droops in what I interpret as shame. I have begun the painful chore of packing and am presently bogged down in my childhood collection of bubble gum cards. I leaf through these faces once so important to me. Feeling a time-tarnished version of the old thrill. I, who throw away nothing, must now cram the most practical, and therefore boring, of my goods into that ugly pack. And leave all else behind. With my things, I leave this room. With the room, I leave the house. With the house, the yard. The yard, the fields. The fields, the farm. And so on to the limits of my homeland. To join an army of faceless refugees. I can't say that I would feel better if it was a war that was chasing me away. But I would certainly feel less animosity at myself if it was something I hadn't caused.

I walk to the window and look out through the long-yellowed curtain that preceded me here. There is wind today. Not one of the unrecorded hurricanes, but a steady breeze that barely wiggles our poplar windbreak. The trees give up their frosted leaves more willingly now.

My father walks across the yard carrying a block of salt. I used to share those blue bricks with the cattle. Unbothered by fear of dirt and germs. Mother, having more sophisticated fears, told me that the magpies shit on the salt blocks. It broke me of the habit. But for the next year or so, the cattle must have suffered a salt deficiency as I dutifully shooed them away from the polluted blocks as well.

It is definitely a Peter Pan mood that's upon me this day. I never decorated the walls of my room in teenage fads. I left it wearing my childhood. Prizes from the penny bubble-gum machine, threaded with string, are hung on the wall. A coloured picture of Jean Beliveau, tattered now. Part of a series I collected from a weekend magazine. Religious ornaments. A portrait of St. Theresa hangs framed in a plastic doily. That was a present from the sisters when I was recovering from appendicitis. I served Mass in the hospital chapel each morning and they thought I had a certain vocation for the priesthood. Admit to feeling guilt-ridden when the talk, back in the room, got dirty. Those discovering days in a hospital full of older people. The climax being the day the sick lady hobbled down the corridor with the back of her gown undone. My first glimpse of adult nudity. In those days when even pregnancy was a spicy item of chat.

I stuff a few items in my pack and it seems full. Will have to stand nude at the laundromat. If such a thing exists there. What a pathetic pastime all this is! I flop back onto my bed. To sit here weeding this garden which I perceive to have no weeds. Throwing out the pansies of the past. I close my eyes and, with just a bit of encouragement, fall gratefully to sleep.

5: Cultural Differences A: Communication

WHEN I awake, the late summer sun has already set. I try desperately to go back to sleep. Rather than face the evening, I would love to sleep until tomorrow. Marathon-style. Hoping only for sympathetic dreams. But I am treasonously awake. Even the old sheep-counting standard fails to make me even drowsy.

Eventually, fear of bedsores pushes me out onto my feet. I trundle down the stairs and into the kitchen, about which Mother stampedes in an unusual tizzy.

"I went to the store and forgot all about your father's lunch! He must be starving!"

Sandwiches being flopped together with great dispatch. My mother working with an inhuman quota of hands. "Tyrone, would you mind terribly taking this out to him?"

"Terribly." She looks at me. The water tanker supplying her eyes about to pump. "Just kidding, Mom."

With a grin, I grab the lunch box.

"You're sleeping an awful lot lately, Tyrone. Don't you feel well?"

"Feel like a charm, Mother. Just preparing my body for the journey. Don't want to get sick over there. You know, the doctors are supposed to be a little primitive. "

"Oh, dear."

"Not to worry, Mother. I'm practically invincible. After all, I do calisthenics. Bye now."

Out into the dropping night. Mother left fingering her cheek with worry. Thinking I am so brave. I am so brave that when my own dog barks, I convulse with fear and walk into the side of my truck.

"Nice Plato."

I pat his black head and wonder if he asks himself why I am shivering. His tongue out a foot and his tail wagging. Not much competition for the title of this man's best friend.

"Not nice to leap out at me barking like that. Might have a heart attack. Then no more kind master, Plato. No more dog biscuits dropped out the window at midnight. Sit Plato."

Plato sits. His ears go flat to his head. A sulk and sadness in his eye. Associates any kind of order with cruelty. Thinks he's being reprimanded. Smart Plato, I think. I have never been fond of orders myself.

Plato was with me the day of the great gassing. When I almost got us both killed. He doesn't come with me any more. Thinks I'm going to lead him again to poisoned air. I should sue again. This time for the loss of the trust of an old friend.

On that fateful day, I led poor, frolicking Plato across a pipeline, which happened to be leaking massively underground. Both of us took several lungfuls and collapsed in heaps near by. We were discovered shortly and rushed off to our respective hospitals, where we recovered slowly amid much publicity. A reputable lawyer sued the responsible company heavily on my behalf. I won both a lump sum settlement and a compensatory income when a team of doctors discovered that my sense of smell was missing and unaccounted for.

Funny that when the money rolled in from the lawsuit, I thought it was the beginning of great things. And now it is just another item facilitating my departure. It knocked down a hurdle which I would give possibly a finger to rebuild. And they call me lucky. All wish that they were in my shoes. To anyone I would give that privilege. They could have my mind for no extra charge. Must go, Plato. And drop biscuits off for Father.

My truck rumbles over the gravel, leaving a con trail of dust behind. Just dark enough for lights. Just light enough that they don't do any good. Good time of the evening for hitting skunks. Did that once. Drove on as fast I could go. Avoided that road for weeks. Didn't want to see a trace of what I'd done. The stink clung to my tires for a long time. The smell of guilt.

The thought of killing makes me physically ill, but there's no noble reason for it. Just my usual cowardice. I find it easy to identify with the beast in the bead of the hunter's gun, or the skunk beneath my wheels. Ran off the road into a ditchful of snow once, so as not to hit a rabbit that had trapped himself in my headlights. He stood up on hind legs for a minute or two to watch my ridiculous efforts to regain the road. Then hopped ungratefully away.

Full of funereal thoughts, I drive. Imagining the singing of the souls of beasts. Just another overwrought noise from my truck. Still, I wonder if they watch us from somewhere. Is the skunk's soul out there somewhere saying, "There's the lousy bastard that cut me down in my prime."

Perhaps the whole state of my affairs is his revenge.

Now down an approach and along packed dirt tracks. The light in the distance is Father. Going around and around. Often wondered what is in his mind when he is out there. Perhaps he has found an exquisite peace for reason of which he does not retire. A peace that excludes all thoughts and hums a tranquil tune. I park and wait for him to come around. The roar approaches. He stops, pushes up the throttle, and in a few seconds the motor dies. Letting in a syrupy solitude. The sort of silence that reminds you how noisy the mind is. I listen to a thought being processed. The door opens. My dusty-faced father climbs in.

"I brought your lunch." He opens the bucket and pokes his finger at a sandwich.

"The hell with it. Take me home."

Is that a note of frustration I just heard? If so, the first ever. Start up, U-turn, and back from the field we go. Father hunched and silent.

"I think I'm going to retire."

"Why?"

I am amazed. Thought time stood still for Father. "I don't think you'd understand. That's a switch, isn't it?"

"Try me."

Possibly the first eagerness he has ever heard from me.

"All this used to be fun. I didn't used to give a shit whether I harvested the stuff or not. Just liked watching it grow. And now, I don't give a damn about anything but the money. Sometimes I look across those fields and I think that everything out there but me is stone dead. I'm sick of having that lousy tractor for company."

He speaks slowly. Dejection dripping off each word.

"You're not going to do anything like this, are you?"

"Farm? I doubt it. I'd starve to death."

"Probably. What are you going to do then? I don't really care, but I'm curious."

"Don't you care at all?"

He laughs. "No. Not really."

"I don't know what I'm going to do."

"I didn't think so."

No more words pass. I sit wishing he hadn't said he didn't care. When I leave, that will be one more unhappiness. Knowing that not even my father cares if I return. Can't blame him for feeling that way, I guess. Can damn well blame him for saying so. Foolish of me to think that he, like Mother, would carry a little pin in his heart for me. Inscribed: my son, for better or worse. Father is too practical. Everything cut and dried. No room for irrational likings. Laughable that I would think he cared. After all, not the type to go limpid-eyed over a blood relation. Even Uncle Alfred, his sole, surviving brother, he only good-naturedly puts up with.

God! That leaves so few who do care. My childhood friends have grown up to be catskinners and farmers. Who joke about me with each other and with the older generation over glasses of draught beer. My university friends no doubt cancelled me from their memory ledgers the day I left the place. Perhaps my name gets a shuffle during the reminiscing of a particularly good Revel-squeezing excursion. But, why should they go so far as to care?

Mother cares, of course; but she would care the same amount about anyone or anything that bore the title of her son. Her emotion is too impersonal to be counted. And now my father adds himself to the list of those who've turned away. Is there anyone left? Just my sweet Athena. My Eve who may also get bored with the garden. Go seeking other more interesting Adams in the deserts beyond. At the moment she remains apparently devoted. But seeing nothing in myself to warrant it, I feel insecure. I will try to keep her entrenched in her ignorance, but I'm not entirely sure how to begin.

It's a bit like being an infant who sees a house built of playing cards. He thinks it is pretty. Yet, he doesn't know what he can or can't do to the house. He wants to blow in it, but is afraid. The first attempt he makes to do anything with the house, it does fall down and he cries and perhaps feels that the world has no mercy. But it wasn't enough just to look at the house. He had to involve himself in a stronger way. And so it is with me not knowing the mechanics of Athena's love. I can't touch that love for fear it will vanish before my hand, but I can't not touch it either. The child will take heart when someone troubles to build him a new house of cards. But no one can build me a new Athena! And I don't trust the world to bring me a reasonable replacement either. So I grip onto the thought of Athena with tenacity, while the reality of Athena does as it pleases. All I can hope is that, by continuing the current balance of revelation, deception and fabrication in my personality, I remain what she desires.

We arrive back in the farmyard. My father dejected and I depressed. My mother wondering if the world on the other side of the hill has been struck by disaster. A silent and mournful evening begins.

Mother says over supper, in an attempt to cheer, "Why don't we have a farewell party for you this weekend, Tyrone?"

"Who would come?"

Mother again quiet. The clock ticks audibly. Smashing the silence with seconds. More fun than a wake. I go to the living room. Guitar or TV?

"Lots of people!" Mother's dish-drying silhouette in the door.

"Lots of people what, Mother?"

"Lots of people would come." Lots for my mother could be anything in excess of three.

"Athena, Uncle Alfred, Holly and Pete, Hughie and Adelaide. Just lots of people."

"Mother, Uncle Alfred and Holly and Pete don't like me."

"They'd come."

"Mother, I don't want your friends coming to say goodbye to me."

I hear a sniff. I have apparently struck one of the several hundred notes in Mother which inspire her to tears.

"Our friends aren't good enough for you, I suppose. They haven't fancy educations. They're just simple dirt farmers. Just dirt to you, I suppose."

"No, Mom, it's not that way at all. It's only that there doesn't seem to be much sense inviting people who dislike me to say goodbye to me."

"You've never bothered to get to know them, that's all."

Time to retreat and agree to her terms. I wonder if she misunderstands purposefully to ensure that she gets her way.

"As you wish then, Mother."

She will now ask me if I'm sure in order to free herself of any guilt.

"Are you sure? After all, it's you that's leaving. You shouldn't have to do anything you don't want."

"That's fine, Mother. Invite anyone you like."

Invite Stewart Thomson and his wife so they can whisper about me behind the backs of their hands. Invite Norbert Foley and maybe he'll sing that song about his "Fightin' Side" again. Perry Bolton too. I love how he yanks my hair and says, "Look at all this shit." It's such fun when he chases me around with his jackknife. Really, Mother, I wouldn't miss it for the world.

I shouldn't have to do anything I don't want. That's a good one. Can't remember the last time I actually did anything that I wanted to do. I don't want to go to Europe. I don't want to drive when it's windy. And now, I don't want to have a lousy farewell party. But go ahead. The machinery of this world has a way of churning on anyway, as I yank frantically on the emergency-stop chain. What is one more inconvenience in my life which counts time in terms of them?

Mother leaves, excited. Making plans. Probably to bake pastries. For this excuse to have a big friendly reunion. Fill the house with people. Pour out the beer in buckets. Inspired conversations about climate, crops, and provincial politics. While I sit alone. Everyone having already asked me their token questions.

Where are you going first? What will you do? How travel? What company? Why leave? When leave? When return? Why return? What do when return? What future? And then a "that's so nice" and a "wish you luck." And an "excuse me but I left my husband holding my beer."

The incredible hypocrisy of everyone everywhere!

There's only the small consolation that if people didn't bother pretending to be considerate, they would be even more unbearable.

I can't watch TV with my mind this full of human failure. Too cynical to elevate this detective to superhumanism. Am caught picking apart his acting. Snorting at the stereotyped script. So sad to have let myself be caught up in this hobby of armchair cynics everywhere. Where a garden becomes not the flowers, but the weeds which sneak between. Snap the TV black and sit in darkness. My mind a blank white screen. Projector light, but no images. The entrances out of which thoughts flow all laboriously plugged. My eyes slam shut even on the moonlight. Nothing is as safe and quiet now as my mind made vacant. The faintest hint of melancholy music. Just enough to tinge the emptiness with a faint hue of bitterness. Time stands still for me while it crawls on for others. I revel in exquisite boredom.

6: Cultural Differences B: Sports and Other Pastimes

THURSDAY. I woke up saluting it as if it were the last one ever. Might be. For me that simple cycle may forget to start over again. Tomorrow is the party. Mother on the phone madly all morning. Receiving many regrets. Previous commitments. But, unfortunately, a few also who would love to come. Thinking no doubt, "I'd say farewell to a pogo stick for free beer and food." Athena cannot come. Already promised to work overtime that night. Her boss, damn his faulty heart, doing his utmost to trap her alone in the empty building. Not as old as I had thought either. Only sixty-three. Might still be able to convert the odd lewd thought into a shaky action. I told Athena I forbade it and she laughed. Thought I was joking. Left it at that for fear she' d think me ridiculous. Fine time I will have at the party fantasizing his wrinkled hands darting toward her body!

Uncle Alfred, of course, can come. Deaf as a beet and hobbling on his cane, he wouldn't miss it for the world. Would walk miles through molten cat shit to get to someone willing to listen to his life story. For one lousy motive or another, everyone except me will be glad to be there.

Lunchtime now. Phone interrupting. Mother leaping to answer. It is one of her golden moments. The phone ringing itself off the wall symbolizes her power in the community. She is the centre of attention and is loving it by seconds. Choosing the evening's company.

The baking bread smoking our eyes. Dough swelling along the counters like fat flesh. Not the peace and quiet I had dreamt of for these last days. Must get away. Out where living things are silent and sensible about their societies. I wipe crumbs from my lips and excuse myself from the table. I go and collect my gear box and fishing rod. I start for the door.

Father likes to see me with rod and reel. A more normal habit than most of mine.

"Off fishing, are you?" he says.

"No. Actually I'm going to chop down a tree." For the moment the fact I am going fishing outweighs the fact that I'm a smartass and Father continues.

"Where are you going to try?"

"Below the spillway about a quarter mile."

"You won't catch anything there on a day like this. If you were going to fish there you should've been out at four this morning."

"Is that a law? I mean, can I go there or do I have to go to my MP and have it ratified in Parliament."

"Go ahead, but it's a waste of time. The fish are onto that spot. It's been fished to death. They're feeding way down the river now. You should try it down by Miller's bridge. Sam hates trespassers. Takes his shotgun after them. The fish should be as thick as hair on a dog there."

"Not worth getting shot over."

"Sam only takes pot shots at outsiders. He wouldn't bother you."

"I don't think he'd think of me as the Beaver Creek in-crowd."

"Don't be stupid. He's not apt to shoot you today when he's coming to your party tomorrow night."

Might be all the more tempted, I think. Wipe out the only blemish on a perfect evening.

"Is Sam coming for sure?" I grimace.

"I would imagine. He's never turned down a free beer yet."

Sam Miller who has never officially recognized my existence. If I stand between him and whoever he's talking to, he stares through me as if I was air. He does unofficially recognize me, however. Whenever I am there, he turns the subject of conversation around to those "lazy SOBs who come out of university with their smart-ass degrees and would sooner starve than do an honest day's work. And they're all stupid as duck eggs about commonsense things."

"Sam Miller hates my guts. Why is he coming?"

"I already told you. To drink free beer."

"Couldn't we send him a bottle in the mail?"

"I like Sam."

"It's my party."

"Well, you phone him up then and say that he can't come."

"All right, he can come. And drown himself for all I care!"

I start again for the door. Father only speaks when you're trying to leave.

"What kind of bait are you going to use?"

"Flies."

"You must be joking."

"I'm not joking. I'm going to use flies."

"That's stupid! Fish won't go for flies today. It's worm weather. Any damn fool knows that. You should go out and dig some worms."

"I don't want to use worms. I want to use flies!"

"Go ahead! Use flies all day if you want. You're just too bloody lazy to dig. I don't give a damn if you waste all day flicking flies at fish that want worms. You never catch anything anyway!"

"Goodbye."

"You think you know everything. If you tried listening once in a while, you might catch a fish. And you might quit smashing up my machinery too!"

The last dig.

"What brought that on?"

"You should know. You did it. For Chrissake, don't play stupid. I saw you do it."

"Do what?"

"Smash up the lawn mower, that's what!"

"That was an accident."

"It's always an accident with you. You might've known that if you ran the lawn mower over the rock path you were going to break the blade. Those things cost money, you know."

"How much? I'll pay you for it."

"It's not just the price. It takes time to put the damn thing in as well."

"I'll buy it and put it in."

Father laughs. "You'll put it in like hell. You couldn't put a handgrip on a bicycle."

Mother walks in. These arguments mortify her. Chisel into her dreams of a happy, inseparable family.

"Do you two have to argue? Couldn't you get along for just three more days? Is that too much to ask?" There is a dramatic lull.

"If he smashes up one more thing of mine he can leave sooner!"

"He was doing you a favour, Tom. He was mowing the lawn."

"Well, he does a lousy job, and he probably broke the mower on purpose because he was bored and didn't want to finish."

"I should have run it over your foot!"

Mother, like a true dove, steps between, screaming "Stop it!" I turn and leave. Always ready to turn tail and run from a nasty situation.

Things have a way of going from bad to much worse. Yesterday it appeared that Father merely might not care that I was leaving. Today it looks as if he's impatient for it to happen.

I start the long walk to the river. It doesn't matter where I fish, to tell the truth. Or what bait I say I use. I don't really fish in the fisherman's sense. I fish in an ornamental sense. Don't use bait. Don't use a hook. Just tie on my special leader (when no one's near by) – two weights and a lure with no hook attached. In our community, you can't just say that you are going to sit on the river bank. People would say you were weird and lazy. But if you have a fishing rod in your hand while you're sitting on the river bank, you are recognized and admired as a sportsman. No one knows my secret. They all think I'm just a lousy fisherman.

I would hate to ever catch a fish. To yank it out of the water by sneaking treachery. Laugh with my fellows as I held it up by its flapping gills. Smack its head on a rock. That's if I was a gentleman. Throw it live in a basket to writhe and suffocate for hours if I wasn't. Maybe shove a stick through its gills. Could never do any of that with my great fears of death and dying.

I certainly chomp them down with relish though. Also pet cows and then eat beefsteak for supper. The great contradictions in all our lives. Saying "my, what a pretty calf" as if we were as oblivious of its fate as it is itself. Could become a vegetarian. And quit swatting flies. But what good is even that when a scientist somewhere has recently discovered that flowers feel pain. We are all thoroughly dependent parasites. Differing degrees of same. From bloodthirsty hunter down to self-righteous vegetarian. Burdening the world. Applying to nature for relief. Everyone should feel guilty for being at all.

And then there are the ecologists. Perhaps the most dangerous of all human parasites. For they have taken it upon themselves to show man a way to erase his guilt. To fit him into the great balance. With angelic expression, they ride their bicycles and eat organic food. (Deaf to its weeping.) They print their Bibles for the twentieth century, complete with commandments. All so eager to survive. Personally see little sense in going hairy over the survival of future generations. Can't see all that much sense in preserving this one. Besides myself, of course.

Down this coulee I walk. The grass is frosty-brown these days. This place I have loved since little-boyhood. Carried a .22 then. Much as I carry my fishing rod now. Would set up tin cans just around the bend from here and blast off a few shells at them. Would come home with brags of killing different things. Whatever I had seen, I would claim to have killed. Father beat me severely on the ass for killing a hawk one day. Of course I hadn't. Hadn't even shot near it. But claimed to have dropped it when it was just a tiny speck in the sky. Didn't know Father was so fond of hawks. He said it was a stupid thing to do. That they killed mice. Mice chew the strings off of hay bales. I, personally, couldn't even kill mice. Used to shut my eyes when Father smashed them dead with his great boots, when he found them living in the hay stooks.

The coulee winds its way down to the river, usually bearing some kind of water. Fed by springs, it only dries up in very dusty summers. It's such a comforting bit of water. Never over your gum boots when you wade down it. Little three-foot waterfalls. Easily imagined into Niagaras. There are tracks of animals in the snow drifts that pile over it in winter. Four trees exactly from here to the river. Their roots eroded bare, like fingers straining to hold onto their perch.

I'm saying goodbyes, as I go. Here, two other coulees enter and the little stream grows bigger. From here on, whisky bottles lie stranded on the shores. The old fellow who lived at the top of one of these coulees was a notorious rye drinker. He pitched his empty bottles into the coulee and, each spring, when the water rose, they scattered toward the river. He is long dead, but his bottle legacy lives on.

Each step of this journey is so familiar. Like an old friend. The only things I have had to truly count on. Again on the verge of a sniffling "O Canada." Am so sick of reasons for why I am like this. Incapable of sensible explanation, I can only moan like something wounded.

Now at the river. The valley suddenly opening wide. I gravitate to my favourite spot. Flop down in the damp. I shiver. Little heat in this fall sun. The wind rakes through the trees like fingers. Combing out the leaves. Three days left. The time already crippled with parties.

It was near here where I walked into that pocket of gas. Maybe I should return there and stamp around. In hopes that another puff will rise and send me to hospital. No. No sense dreaming of timely disasters. The future leaping out of the shadows to say, "Boo! Thought you were going to do that, eh? Fat chance! Your future's over here. Dark and dim."

This is the famous Beaver Creek for which our Post Office was named. The legend is that a Scottish pioneer christened it when he discovered a beaver, belly-up and smelling, in a rock-sheltered eddy.

I look over to the place on the far bank where rails stick out of the cliff. They are mine-car rails. An ancient prospector had a gold mine right there. What became of him is hard to say, but his mine was blasted shut after two children lost themselves in it for a day and a half. We used to swim below it and those braver than I walked out to the rails' end to dive. Hard to imagine him plumbing a tiny seam of gold deep in that hill. Descending into the damp blackness each day. Pushing out a car of ore each evening. To shake and sift for glittering bits. Then to lie smoking his pipe on lamplit evenings, cold and alone.

I am all the present day has to offer this crook of river bottom, so deeply steeped in history. It will sit in unfair loneliness when I am gone. It is one hundred and twenty miles southwest of Calgary, the next big city. Land location: the southeast quarter of section thirteen, range twenty-nine, township four, west of the fourth meridian. For most of our province's residents, and certainly for the rest of the nation, it might as well be on the moon.

I cast my line into the river's middle. I pick a spot, a rock above the water line. And compete with myself to drop my harmless lure near to it. They have competitions like this in official circles. I saw one once on TV. Have little coloured rings of various sizes that the competitors must cast into. Vary the distance to determine the champion. I divide myself into three parts: the reigning champion, the umpire, and myself. He casts. I cast. At various targets chosen by the umpire. If he comes closer, I do a little arbitrary switching. I exchange the me that is he for the me that is me. So that I always win. Not always, really. Sometimes, at uncrucial points in the match, I let his victories stand. To add spice to the contest.

Now the game draws to an end. Very closely matched in points, we arrive at the final target. The water weeds fifty feet downstream. Best of three. I cast very poorly. He casts closer. One for the bad guy. (Who, by the way, has exposed a number of very creepy characteristics during the course of this championship.) I win the second round. "Take that, you sod." This is it! The tie-breaker. The rubber. He casts well. Two feet off. Undaunted, I cast. Whoops! Twenty feet at least from the weeds. But wait! There's been a foul! Apparently he stepped over the restraining line. The bastard! We'll do it all over again. He casts. Ha! Ha! What a joke! He almost missed the river. I cast. Much nearer. Almost right into them. The victory is mine. He breaks his rod over his knee. Lousy sport. I am crowned King of the Target-Casting World. Kissed on the cheek by Miss World 1972. Shake hands with the Prime Minister who asks if I'll give him private lessons. I say that I'll see if I have time at the end of the season.

Now, not yet tired of my game, I invent a new, even more venomous challenger. He lays a million dollars on the line to play me. I take him up on it. We start again. I cast. Go to reel back in. A jerk! For a heart-stopping second, I think I have caught a fish. God knows how. I pull. My line is wound in a brush pile across the stream. I yank this time. And again. Nothing. I walk up and down. Pulling my line this way and that. One more mighty try and snap! The weightless line drifts back to me. I curse and kick the stones. My best lure. Gone forever.

It was such a pretty thing; bright red with golden stripes. I always hoped that the fish down there were having fun chasing it around. And now it's gone. I won't take the hook off another one. The World Champion will merely retire undefeated.

I look out to that pile of wood in which my line and lure are knotted. What the hell, I finally decide. Better to leave it there, a little memento of departed me, than have it and its secret discovered by my parents.

The sun is bearing down on the hills now. Soon to plunge behind them. Time to say a last farewell. Hope no one's watching me blow kisses to the hills. Back to the coulee mouth now.

For the climb to the top. Walk back on the other side. Always do it that way. Changes the scenery entirely. Farewell Beaver Creek. If only I can live to see you again. I'm very glad I left the lure behind now. Only wish I could have done it by my own volition. Ceremoniously chucking it into midstream while mouthing Latin. Oh well. When did my life ever wait to consult me before going ahead on its own?

7: Cultural Differences C: Politics

AND THE criminal goes off handcuffed to his just deserts. Bravo! Now a beans commercial. They'll make you big and strong, boys and girls. And they'll make you lose friends. And be little laughingstocks when your little sphincters forget during busy recess. What comes now, I wonder? I never consult viewing guides. Spoils the excitement. No chance to say, "Perfect, just what I wanted to see." And you'd never be able to snap the set off in disgust either.

Station identification. "This is the CBC," they say. And I say, "Get on with it; I know that." Another commercial. Sexy girls in microscopic bikinis strolling a beach drinking a soft drink. Camera zooming in on their bosoms, then on the brand name on the bottles. Then sliding down their bronze thighs like a cautionless playboy's eye. Perhaps they are intending to show that drinking this particular soft drink makes you grow a voluptuous bosom. Also acts as a suntan lotion when applied externally. Now one of these dolls is chewing a tall, dark, and handsome's ear as the sun crashes crimsonly into the ocean. She holds up a bottle of Brand Y and winks at all of us out in TV land. So we'll know that Brand Y is an aphrodisiac and tastes great after a meal of raw ear. The camera zooms up and away. The scene glints gold. The couple now a tiny black silhouette. Bravo!

The moment of truth. Oh god! Another special on the federal election. I walk to the set. Will snap it off in disgust. A brass band plays "O Canada." Well-spiced with cymbals. All in very bad taste. Just as my finger reaches the machine's trigger, I hesitate. I draw back. The election! Why didn't I think of that before? (Possibly because I never read newspapers.) I sit back down. Watching avidly. What a great plan is assembling in my mind! I have an undisputed right to vote; so why not vote? This could be my greatest deception of all time. After all, I am not completely ignorant of politics. I know the three major parties and their leaders' names. Of course, I will have to know a little more than that to convince everyone that the election is a matter of life and death to me.

I stare at the TV ravenous for knowledge. The ultra-objective network commentator is running down different aspects of the election. He has one eyebrow uncomfortably raised all the while. I try it. It hurts and is difficult to sustain. Perhaps it was this particular talent that enabled him to rise so high with the CBC. I memorize his lines. Soon I will be an authority.

Now they are taking closer looks at individual constituencies. The plot thickens. I watch closely for a glimpse of our constituency. Will be difficult to pull this off without knowing who is running here. No news of anything west of Winnipeg. Where the Eastern world stops. I sneak out into the kitchen and dig through the pile of papers.

"What are you looking for?" My every movement is monitored.

"This week's *Western Press.*" I continue digging. Mother has left for a women's club meeting and Father feels free in her absence to be as obnoxious as he pleases.

"Are you actually going to read it or do you need something to file your nails onto?"

"I happen to be quite keen about the news."

"If you're so damn keen, you'd know that this week's *Press* doesn't get here until tomorrow."

"The way you hog it I never get to see it until it's a week old."

I finally find last week's.

"Catch any fish?"

"Several."

He laughs. I leave.

Digging frantically through the paper. It looks like it's all ads. Where in hell do they put the news?

"The crossword puzzle is on page thirty-seven," Father yells from the kitchen.

Full of humour tonight. Funny as epilepsy. Oh, here it is. Right at the front. All sorts of election news. Ahah! Rocky Mountain South. I'm sure that's what our riding is called. I read ferociously. Lionel Austin is the Liberal. Horst Procowitz is the Conservative. No one is running for the NDP. The little article is finished. That should be all I need to know. I marvel at how boring news is. Hard to believe people shoot one another because of it. Am tempted to do the crossword. I turn to page thirty-seven. Father already has.

I am much cheered up. If this works, I could possibly figure my way out of this mess entirely. I rehearse my act. Oh, if it only works. Must sleep tonight with fingers crossed and my rabbit's foot beneath my pillow. Perhaps it shouldn't all occur in one day though. Should warm up to the punch line slowly. Where's Father when I need him? He seems to have gone out. I sit listening for him to come in, drinking in more election gossip from the tube as I wait. I hear the door. Now for Phase One.

Father stands in the porch, garbed in parka and coveralls.

"I think that goddamn milk cow is going to calve tonight. I've got enough bloody things to do without having to stay up all night midwifing that bitch."

"How do you think the election's going to go?"

"Huh?" Father looks at me quizzically.

"The election. How do you think its going to turn out?"

"A Liberal landslide."

"On the contrary, I think the Conservatives are going to come up very strong in the upcoming election. Labour is very uneasy under the present Liberal regime and I think you will find it shifting its support on a nationwide scale."

"Look, you instant political genius, the Conservatives know about as much about politics as you do and that is why they're going to get stomped as usual."

"Perhaps you have underestimated the unsettling effect of the NDP campaign. While people may not be willing to swing their votes to the left, the NDP campaign may have convinced them to move their votes somewhere. Therefore, a conservative win may be in the offing."

"What in hell is with you? Why don't you go watch TV or read your comics or something."

A low blow.

"I'm sorry, Father. I thought you were interested in politics."

"I am. But that doesn't mean that I have to be interested in what my stupid son has to say about it."

Father is not responding as I had hoped. Seems to be in an extremely obnoxious frame of mind. Thought he was a Conservative. Only two choices and I chose wrong. My luck is truly rotten. However, I am not as of yet too deeply committed. Never too late to switch ideologies, I have often noticed.

"Still the Liberal strength cannot be denied. Trudeaumania and charisma are powerful weapons still. And the government's work in the area of international diplomacy does deserve a certain amount of credit." Father turns crimson.

"If that bastard would've spent a little more time on internal diplomacy, he might've done something about peddling that mountain of wheat I've got rotting in the bin!"

Wrong again. So my father's a Socialist. Never would have thought it. But having now zeroed in, I can really begin the snow job.

"The NDP are really putting up a brilliant campaign, aren't they?"

"That bunch of goddamn reds couldn't put up a pillow fight."

Perhaps Father doesn't vote.

"Who are you going to vote for?"

"None of your goddamn business." He looks at his watch.

"Jeez! I've blown half an hour in this stupid conversation. If that cow's calving and anything's gone wrong, I'm going to wring your neck." Father backs into the night.

Often, he is not a sweet person. He has certainly planted himself in the path of my plan. Still, his encouragement and interest in my sudden love of politics aren't vital to its success. Would have helped, but won't scuttle it.

Father re-enters, puffing with exertion.

"Calf's backwards. I need your help. Right now, so don't fart around getting down to the barn." I pull on my boots and charge after him. Coatless. What bravery! I arrive at the barn right behind him.

"Goddamn cow! After this many calves she should know how to do it right."

The hooves are showing; bottoms up. That's how you tell if the calf is backwards. There are many reasons to be upset in such a situation. The calf's hair is smoothed from head towards tail, so that when he arrives backwards, his own hair obstructs his passage. The cow cannot push as well either because her muscles are working with the grain of the hair instead of against it. Consequently no traction and the calf might lie caught until he drowned.

That is the other problem: drowning. When the calf is born normally, head first, his nose is well out when the umbilical cord breaks and he must take his first breath of air. But when he backs his way into the world, it sometimes breaks with his nose still buried. He draws in the fluid and is born dead or drowning. My father slips the looped ends of our calving string over the hooves and tightens them above the hocks. We begin to pull. An easy, steady pull.

"Jeez! He isn't budging. She must've been bred by an elephant. If we lose this bloody calf, I'm going to quit!"

We pull a little harder. Must be careful not to reef. Could easily cripple him.

"Shit! I'm going for the winch. Keep a steady pull so we don't lose any ground. He's a goner by now. Damn the luck. This lazy bitch has quit pushing altogether."

Father tears out of the barn. I have begun to sweat keeping up this steady tension. I move so that I am pulling down, more toward the cow's feet. Then, for no apparent reason, the calf's hips slip past and with a sucking sound he falls out into the world. His sides are still but his heart beats. He will die in no time if he doesn't breathe. His nostrils flare as he tries to force air into his collapsed lungs. I pump one front leg quickly to try and get him breathing. Nothing. I grab his slimy back legs and hold him up by them. Shaking him. A slow drool pours from his mouth. His lungs are crammed with liquid. I kick over the waterbarrel in the corner and roll him back and forth along it. At last I hear a gurgling in his throat as a bit of air finds its way into his sodden lungs. I continue to roll him and the gurgling gets louder as the air reaches deeper into him. Father comes in, arms full of pulley and rope. Drops all and kneels down to fish the slime from the calf's throat.

"He's a big one, eh?" I nod.

"He's all right now, I think. He can get the rest of that crap out by himself."

Father drags the calf over by its mother who lies still, flat on her side.

"Up, you useless bitch!"

He kicks her. She rears her head up and rolls onto her feet in a second. Bawls a warning.

"Something tells me we should get the hell out of here."

I am out the door. Father pushes past me. The old cow inside paws at the straw and sniffs and licks her coughing calf. We walk back to the house.

Funny that assisting cows in this respect doesn't bother me. Matter of conditioning, I suppose. Still I haven't managed to condition myself to any other type of gore. The difference is obvious, I guess. For those who can discern between life and death. Something always magical about calves popping out and beginning to breathe. By lending my hand to it, I niggle a part in the miracle. Like being an extra in a great movie. I lost most everything in that simile. Some things just aren't like anything.

I go to the living room. The hell with the Plan. It can wait. For this small while, I can lock out all unpleasantness. Because I have something nice, for a change, to saturate the thinking space. Father is no longer aggressive. He too sits in satisfaction. Perhaps even pleased with my performance. More likely happy that his problems have diminished by one while his assets have increased the same. He sits smoking and staring in the kitchen. I sit smoking and staring in the living room. We are both the same kind of happy because of the same event. But we could never traverse that short distance to be that way together.

After a long while, Father ambles by, yawning and scratching. Bedroom bound. He pauses at the door and says between yawns, "By the way, Tyrone, if you're thinking of sneaking out of going to Europe by telling us that you feel it's your national duty to stay and vote, you'd better forget it. People pre-ballot by the hundreds every election because they aren't going to be around on election day. Goodnight."

Father disappears into his bedroom with, I swear, the hints of a grin playing around his whiskers. Leaving the Plan ever so slightly in ruins.

8: Cultural Differences D: Food, Drink, and the Party

DRIFTING HELPLESSLY in inner space. In my living room which is so perversely lit up. Robbed of its darkness which I cherish so. And worse than that, filled with party chairs and card tables. Mother has decided that we will play cards at the party. Quite fitting, playing cards and going to parties being the two pastimes I hate most in this world. Wouldn't want to be happy tonight anyway.

Still, I wish I had been able to choose the setting and situation for my inevitable misery. Wanted the oozing pathos of a dark, lonely room. Got the hectic unhappiness of a brightly lit party. So damn unfair.

The people will be here shortly. Drifting in one by one. I must meet them at the door. Smiling, shaking their hands, saying, "It's so nice of you to come."

Fate has worked paradoxical wonders this night. People who hate me coming to say farewell. Not knowing that their wish-you-wells are like searing sarcasm. Would be so happy if they did know. Hope you have a nice time. Ha, ha. They're not sincere. I'm not sincere. The party standing as the accumulation of maybe a million lies. No one could call it off and the people who are coming couldn't really have done otherwise. Everyone is in a trap of their own setting. If I were not squirming in my own trap, I could sit somewhere laughing hysterically at it all.

Oh, god! I hear voices. At only eight o'clock someone's already here.

"Sorry we're so early, dear. But, I thought I could help you get ready. I know what a chore these things are. How I admire you for taking it on all by yourself."

They have by this time sifted into this room.

"And here's the travelling lad! How are you, Tyrone?"

I get up and walk toward this painted lady. She offers her cheek. I kiss it. Like sticking your face in a box of spices. For an awful second, I am afraid I will sneeze.

"Good evening, Mrs. Horbock. I'm so pleased you could come."

"Oh, call me Holly."

Familiarity has just bred contempt.

"Could I get you a drink, Holly?"

"Not so soon, Tyrone. Maybe later."

Good old Holly brushes by me to deposit her coat. Two social misdemeanours already. Not taking her coat and offering her a drink too early in the evening. Such abstinence mustn't come to her easily. Last time I saw her at a party, she was sitting on my father's knee singing "Home on the Range." Had to be carried to her car by a very red-in-the-face Pete. As I think of him in this humbled state, he swaggers into the living room smoking a cigar. Hard to imagine him blushing or for that matter feeling any kind of emotion. He is yelling weather predictions back to Father, as if the wind consulted him before it blew.

"Howdy, Tyrone. Look at that bloody hair! Holly! Did you see the hair on this young pup? What the hell're you tryin' to prove?"

"That there is little sun on the far side of the moon."

Mother stares at the floor. There is an uncomfortable silence. So few words to create so many diverse feelings in so many people. I see shame, disgust, annoyance, and a pinch of horror. Hold your poses, ladies and gentlemen, while I casually disappear.

"What the hell's that got to do with hair?"

Pete the pragmatist will not let an insane comment pass uncensored.

"Nothing."

"That's what I thought."

Pete has just taught me where the bear shits in the buckwheat. I stand reprimanded.

"Why don't you go get me a beer? You're as tight as your old man. Ha. Ha."

Everyone laughs eagerly. My mental disturbances set aside for later, more private discussion. I tear off for the basement where the stock of beer sits cooling.

Down here in this musty, dimly lit cement hole. Will be the only refuge for me tonight. I sit down on an empty apple box and listen to the mice squeak. Mother never catches any in her traps. The mice pass down, from generation to generation, the secret of extracting the cheese without being caught. Clever little animals. Could probably teach me a helpful lesson if we could converse for a while. My great ability to reason never facilitates my escape. Blinds my instincts as I stumble through the obvious.

Chilly down here. Like a grave. Here we bury the vegetables. I lean over and rip open a case of beer. Take out two. Might as well get smashingly drunk. Dull myself to the pain. Arrive back upstairs, open them, and deliver.

"Well, if Pete's going to start the evening off in style, I shouldn't be the spoilsport." Father too decides not to be a spoilsport.

I give Holly mine. Back to the basement for more. Arrive back upstairs as more people arrive. Give someone mine. Back to the basement. Catch a breather on the apple box. Maybe I should drink mine here. Might otherwise die of thirst. No opener. There on the floor is Mother's gallon jug of cheap sherry for special occasions. Spin the top off. Take a few hearty swallows. Perks me up considerably. Back to the battle.

"Well, there he is, the world wanderer!"

Another row of cheeks to kiss. All this chemistry may give me lip cancer. Shake a few hands. Take a few coats.

"What's all this shit?"

"Hello, Perry! Could I get you a beer?"

"Yeah, bring on the sauce! After we've all had a few, we'll get out the old sheep shears and make short work of this mop. Eh, fellas?"

"Ha. Ha."

Ha. Ha. Everyone's so funny. Back to the basement. Hoist an armful of gallon jug. The sweetest sherry in the world smacks me in the face. Gather a bunch of beers. Back upstairs. Line them up on the counter. Popping off lids with great precision. A blister developing on my thumb. The sherry tickling the inside of my mind with a false heat.

"You're such a brave young fellow, Tyrone! How long will you be gone?"

"About seven years."

"Ah, heavens."

Fight my way out of the lipstick breath.

"Great party, Tyrone! Would you mind cracking me another one? A Blue?"

"Nice of you to come."

People still oozing in. The rooms filling with smoke. Some joker yells, "Fire!" Someone's playing the piano. Norbert Foley's nasal voice. "When you're talkin' 'bout my country, you're steppin' on the fightin' side of me." Back to the basement. Open another case of beer. Another shot of special occasion sherry. Hope no one else wants any.

Mother and Father seem to be lost. Maybe they went to bed. Card game starting in the den. Poker there. Crib in the living room.

"Yeah, get me another one. Maybe it'll improve my luck."

Out into the living room. It heaves and churns like an uneasy stomach. Someone belches sonorously, completing the image.

"Did I ever tell you about the time Billy Blakewell unhitched my horses from my buggy in Beaver Creek?"

"Hello, Uncle Alfred."

"I hopped on my buggy and flicked the reins and the buggers took off like lightning right out of the harness. I was still hangin' onto the leads and got dragged all the way down the street. Ha. Ha."

"I've heard that story about seven hundred times and it bored my ass off every time."

"That's my deaf side, you dumbbell. You have to talk in this ear here. Anyway, the clothes on my front were damn near rubbed through."

"No shit."

"This ear, stupid! The next time I saw Billy I got my own back though."

"I bet you sawed the tongue off his wagon."

"I sawed the tongue off his wagon! Hee. Hee. Hee. No kiddin' now, I sawed the damn thing clean off."

"Would you like a beer, Uncle Alfred?"

"That asshole quack told me I couldn't, but pay no mind to that. You get me one anyway. No siree, I used to drink like anything when I was younger. Poured her down days straight sometimes. Why once . . ."

"Bye-bye."

Should get the old fool one in hopes that he'll have a heart attack. Not nice to think. After all, most of the things I've ever said, which I meant, were directed to Uncle Alfred's deaf ear.

Back to the basement. Sure is a nice party I'm having. I look at my watch. It's only half past nine. This particular ordeal may never end. Until each room is filled with insensitive bodies. May I be the first? A short prayer. Sitting on my apple box. Empty beer cases everywhere. No fear of running out, though. Could fill a swimming pool with Father's reserve. Should smash them all, announce that the beer's gone, and watch the rooms empty within minutes.

Me, my gallon jug, and my apple box. An unholy trinity. A scene from many movies. Should pass out in a heap on the floor, by rights. Apple box on its side. The last dribbles from the jug in a pool beneath my hand. The drunken stupor that always follows a baffling disaster. Would suit my situation admirably. But, at the moment, I, Tyrone Lock, must forge on and upwards. How many beers was I to bring? Who cares? I grab the case. Handing out bottles to begging hands everywhere. Into the poker room.

"You poor bugger. You've been slingin' beer all night. Sit down and play a few hands. Someone will take over."

"I really don't mind."

"Don't play martyr with us. What the hell you drinkin'? You smell like nail polish."

"Sherry."

"Sherry! Ya hear that, boys? He's drinkin' sherry." All laugh. "Is that what they teach you up at college? To swill sherry. Get yourself a man's drink and come and play some poker. I hear that's one thing you college boys get pretty sharp at."

"I don't play."

"What the hell did you say? You don't play poker? Bullshit! You couldn't be your father's son and not know how to play poker."

"Maybe I'm illegitimate."

Everyone looks up at me, mildly censoring. No one minds a naughty remark, but you should never be personal. One of many unwritten community laws. But now that we're on the subject . . .

"Hey, I hear you're takin' a nice-looking chick with you over across the pond."

"Could be a rumour."

"Listen to him, eh boys? I tell you, kid, count your blessings. It's a chance you never would've got in my day. Isn't that right, boys? Lucky if you ever saw a goddamn petticoat back in them days."

All laugh. Soon they'll all be pressing contraceptives into my hand.

"I've got to run." Hurriedly leave. Smack into Father.

"You keeping everyone with full beers?"

"Yes."

Father hasn't been doing too badly himself. His eyes are getting smaller. By the time the night is over they will be little slits.

"I heard what you said to Pete earlier on. You better not be filling anyone else's ears with your weirdo comments."

"Or what? Are you going to make me leave if I do?"

"Don't push your luck, that's all. This party means a lot to your mother and you better not let her down!"

"If I go, you could put on a mask and call it a Hallowe'en party. There's millions of excuses for a party when you think about it."

"Shut up before someone hears you."

"Thanksgiving, or you could burn Uncle Alfred and call it Guy Fawkes Day, or St. Jude's Day, maybe. That would be fitting."

"Oh, hell!"

Father stomps off. I am surrounded by well-wishers. Lying twits, I think. It would be a shame if there was no hell for them all to burn in.

"Well, where are you making for first, Tyrone?"

"Sicily."

"Isn't that where the Mafia comes from?"

"Yes."

"Aren't you frightened?"

"I'm thinking of joining up."

On farther.

"How are you travelling over there, Tyrone?"

"By Chinese junk."

Walking along trying to gain the bathroom. Leaving a crowd of bad feelings behind me.

Finally into the bathroom. Teetering. My system swimming in mother's terrible sherry. I think I am going to be sick. The river threatening to rise. Flood conditions. Alert everyone in the valley. The dam is about to break. Staring down into the white porcelain pool. Better sit down. Head between knees. That helps a bit. What have I been saying? Insulting all the neighbours and friends. Weirdo comments abounding. I can't be sick now and go to bed. Putting the missing piece in everyone's puzzle. He's a lousy drinker too, you know. Got sick at his own party. On sherry. I must quell this rebellion of the body. Down, gorge. Brace yourself, stomach. Clear, head. I stand. Room going around in circle. Close my eyes. A bright swimming darkness. Must do something to knock this drunkenness out of me. Could throw up on purpose. Reduce the amount of alcohol in my system. No protection really. Have tried it before. Just as drunk for a shorter period of time. Throwing up unpleasant. Feel like singing a song. "Roll Me Over in the Clover" comes into my mind. Might attract attention. Could just keep drinking. Hold my stomach down by sheer weight.

"Who the hell's in there, anyway?"

A drunk banging on the door. How uncouth, I think. I jerk open the door. "It is I."

"It's the birthday boy, by Christ."

"It is not my birthday."

The drunken Mr. Tickleman falls by me into the can.

"Well, happy whatever-the-hell-it-is, then."

"Glad you could come, Mr. Tickleman. Mind if I close the door while you pee."

Back into the crowd. Must play my role. Pleased you could come. Could I get you a drink? My you're looking nice tonight. We'll be having lunch soon. Difficult to keep from throwing up when one must say such things.

Father is in front of me again. Hate stares at me from between puffy lids.

"Where the hell've you been? There's people all over needing beers."

"I have been contemplating whether or not to throw up. Pitch the old prunes, one might say."

"You get sick and make a scene and I'll kick your ass up between your ears."

I move off. Father grabs me.

"Where are you going? You go to bed and I'll murder you."

"Heaven forbid, Father. I'm just going shopping for a victim. You don't think I'd toss my biscuits on just anyone's front, do you?"

"You little bastard!"

"Father, someone might hear."

I leave Father standing perplexed and wishing I were dead. Have patience, Father. Your wishes could some day soon come true.

But mustn't let hate for everyone get the best of me. This play hasn't even arrived at its final act. Terrible script. Shakespeare wouldn't have approved of so many climaxes and crises so early. I, the so-thought mad young Hamlet, must wander farther in this labyrinth.

What a joke if all the tunnels were false and not a single one led out. Everyone born to believe that one of these dark alleys will bring you to the prize. All of us so caught up in preconceptions of some grand end of all ends. Might have stumbled over the Truth, or the Way, or the Answer many times and thought it was just another obstacle.

9: Your Voyage Won't Be All Romantic Walks in the Moonlight

WHERE AM I? I am standing staring at the wall. Someone is tapping me on the shoulder. Turn to find it's Muriel, who has changed her name to Melanie.

"What's with you, tiger? Find a Renoir hidden in between the plaster?"

"Hello Muri . . . Melanie. I didn't know you were here."

"Look at you. Drunk as a lord. You barely know you're here. Anyway, I just got here five minutes ago. Your mother said you were in the bathroom."

"I was. In fact, I was thinking of being sick. Why aren't you at university?"

"Couldn't take it any more. All those exams and professors preaching on about the same old stuff. I decided to quit. It's quite a community scandal. I'm surprised you haven't heard."

"No one tells me any gossip. I don't qualify as a link in the Beaver Creek grapevine."

"Beaver Creek grapevine. I like that. Your party's a pain in the ass. Why don't you take me for a walk?"

"I have my duty as this plantation's only slave. Who would serve the drinks?"

"Thought it was your party."

"Just a rumour. Actually it's St. Jude's Day."

"Come on. Take me for a walk. This crowd doesn't need a waiter."

I stumble from room to room looking for an unplugged exit. Good old Muriel. When we were kids, we called her Gazops. I look at them and yes, they are still large by any standards. We used to take turns dating her. The only dark place you could go was the movies. She should be an authority on that particular era of filmmaking. Went off to university on the West Coast. Rumour had it she was pregnant, taking myriad weird drugs and generally coming to no good. Don't like her. But less so than anyone else here. Might as well go for a tour of the barnyard and hear the story of her life. Besides, a good snort of freezing air might bring back my social graces. Out the back door at last. It's about twenty degrees. My breath billows out in white clouds.

"Crap, it's cold out here! You sure pick funny nights to go for walks."

"Come on, tiger, you can handle it. It's a beautiful starry night. The moon's almost full too. Look there's Orion."

Great! Muriel's turned into an astronomy freak.

"So what's happened to you since I last saw you?"

"Shit, you're drunk. You're slurring like anything. What's happened? Ummmm. Had a lot of affairs, one abortion, bombed out of Education one year and quit this year, blew a lot of dope, lived in a West Coast commune last summer. That's about it."

Right on, grapevine.

"So how about you?"

"Nothing really."

"Aw, come on, let's hear the dirt."

"I squeeze the Revels at Safeway's."

"Ha. Ha. You've always had a good sense of humour, Tyrone. That's one thing that can be said for you."

Poor phraseology. Muriel's not too bright. Says what she thinks too often to be thought properly clever.

We are walking toward the barn. Plato joins us, sniffing in naughty places. Clever Plato.

"Been off peeing on all the friends' and neighbours' car tires, Plato? Leaving your little mark? Sending little dog-alphabet messages to the doggies on the other farms?"

"You have a weird mind, Tyrone. Do you do a lot of dope?"

"None. Causes ugly growths on the tips of your ears."

I stumble into the junk pile by the shop. Tear the bottom of one pant leg.

"Jeez, be careful, Tyrone. Man, are you drunk. I'm surprised you weren't running around in there with a lamp shade on your head."

"I prefer swinging on the chandelier and we haven't got one."

"Oh look, you've ripped your pants. Ah, what a shame! Let me see."

Muriel leans down fiddling with my cuff. Stands up unreasonably close to me. Her massive bosoms bullying me backwards. I look down at her sly, grinning face.

"I like your hair, Tyrone. It's getting to the length that I really dig on my men."

She sticks her hands into my sports jacket and slides them up under my arms.

"You've got a far-out body, you know that?"

"What are you doing, Muriel?"

"Don't play stupid, tiger, and my name is Melanie. Do you remember the time you manoeuvred me into that hayloft? Want to try it again? For old times' sake. You might find that I've learned a thing or three hundred."

"I guess you didn't hear about my accident."

"What accident?"

"I fell out of a tree on to a sawhorse." I point down. "No reaction. Sorry."

Muriel stares at me transfixed.

"Oh, my god! How horrible! You poor guy! Oh, like that's terrible, Tyrone. What a bummer! Like I'm really sorry."

"It's all right, Melanie. In time, I will forget and the pain of it all will ease."

We make our way back to the house. Muriel sniffling. Saying she's so sorry.

Don't know why I did that. A lot of people would have jumped at the chance. Maybe I'm faithful. Funny to be so old-fashioned.

I wonder what the sixty-three-year-old businessman looks like. Maybe he's not even stodgy. An aging Italian Casanova. One of the hairy kind. Muscles everywhere from regular workouts at his club. Leaning over the desk at this very minute. Plucking the coil notepad from Athena's hand and tossing it gallantly over his shoulder.

"My little spaghetti bolognaise, it must get lonely out there all by yourself behind that big typewriter. Has anyone told you that your smile lights a room like a beautiful sunrise? Come with me to a little restaurant I know of near here." There will be candlelight, champagne, and then, "You seem to be getting woozy, my little ravioli. Come to my twenty-third-storey apartment that I rent for just such occasions and you can lie down."

Would Athena invent an excuse? Cast him away with a mind full of me?

Back at the house. Into the kitchen. Filled with busy women constructing sandwiches. Muriel red-eyed with grief. Nasty stares from everywhere saying, "What have you done to this poor girl?" Ticklish situation.

"Melanie stepped on a thorn."

Disbelief everywhere. The hell with it. Push on into the living room. Look at my watch. Very slyly. Mustn't let anyone know that time drags. It's only eleven. The party could go on for another two hours.

"Where've you been, you sly dog? Saw you slipping out with Muriel Evans. One's not enough for you, eh? You sly dog."

"We went for a walk."

"Oh, you don't have to make up stories for me, kiddo. I don't judge anyone. To each his own, I say. And good luck. No," he whispers in my ear, "as far as I'm concerned, you should grab at everything you can when you're young. 'Cause you won't be enjoying much by the time you're an old codger like me."

A slap on the back. Passing on his wisdom before he departs from the world.

I sneak into the pantry. Find a bottle of whisky and pour myself a glassful. Mother appears from the crowd as if she were being born. Such a not-nice look on her face.

"What did you do to Muriel Evans? She was crying when you brought her back in from outside."

"She stepped on a thorn, Mother."

I gulp at the burning liquid. Need strength.

"Fat lot of malarkey! Why were you taking her out there in the first place?"

"She asked me to take her for a walk in the first place. So we did."

"I don't approve of this at all, Tyrone. And neither does Mr. Evans. Muriel is sticking up for you, heavens knows why. But Mr. Evans said he has half a mind to knock your teeth in. They're going home, I think. Fine impression you've made on everyone. Getting so drunk and saying nasty things to the company. Then attacking the Evans girl. And why are you drinking more?"

"Oh, Jesus!"

"Don't 'oh Jesus' me! I just thought you would have more sense."

"Do you really want the truth, Mother? The truth about this whole crappy night is that everyone here is plastered. No one came to say goodbye to me. They all came for the free booze. Muriel Evans asked me to take her for a walk and then attacked me. I jilted her and she started crying." Close enough to the truth for present purposes. "All your friends are evil-minded perverts and I got drunk so I could stand their company. At this moment, I would be either sick or asleep if it wasn't that Father threatened to murder me if I did. And that, Mother, that is the truth about this entire abortive evening."

"What awful things to say. You're heartless, Tyrone. You wouldn't think of sparing anyone. You're just trying to make yourself look innocent. All I can ask you is that you quit acting like such a boor for the remainder of the evening. That's all I ask."

"I don't know, Mother. It's difficult for a hardened boor like myself to act like anything else. Bye now."

Is there any hope of even a meagre salvation?

Oh, god! Is that Mr. Evans emerging from the fog? So big, so drunk, so righteously indignant. I squat down and wriggle under Mother's huge fern. My ass sticks out, but it can't be helped. Will he recognize it as mine? Have never thought my ass particularly noteworthy. Someone is kicking my foot.

"All right, Tyrone come out of there. You can't fool me."

His baritone voice resonates throughout the room. I slither out of the fern. Now I will lose my teeth. Have always been so fond of them too.

"I was just plugging in the record player, Mr. Evans."

"My ass! You were hiding. You probably think I'm going to belt you one, don't you?"

"Muriel stepped on a thorn."

"She said she stepped on a stone. Your stories don't even match."

"Oh, Jesus!"

Everyone is crowded around to see my blood spill.

"But look, Tyrone, since Muriel doesn't seem to want you to get belted and since it's your party, I'm going to forget about whatever went on out there. But take a warning, kid, don't make a habit of it."

"Of what?"

"Of whatever the hell went on out there that made my Muriel cry, that's what."

"Oh, Jesus!" Everyone's watching so I think I'll make a speech. "Ladies and gentlemen! I am going to go to bed, but please do not leave. If you haven't already forgotten that this party was for me, please do. It's actually St. Jude's Day, so if you have any complaints, please take them up with St. Jude. Drink as much as you want. It's on my father. If I have managed to insult anyone, please accept my humblest apologies. Good night and 'Es Muchos Caballo.' Which translated into English means, 'It is much horse.'"

I claw my way through the crowd to the upstairs door. Crawl up the stairs and into my room. I take down the key from where it's been hung ever since I can remember. Dusty strings of cobweb stretch away as I move it down to the lock. Wondering if it has ever been used before. The lock springs shut and I manoeuvre clumsily to my bed. Clothes seem to be taking hours to dispense with. In under the sheets at last. With my last crumb of energy, I give the lamp chain a tug. My limbs locked by black quicksand. The whirlpool of night in my mind sucks me down. Then nothing.

10: Have You Someone To Notify in Case of Emergency?

HAVE JUST wakened this Saturday morning with a morning-after stomach. My mouth stuck with noxious glue. Model airplane variety would be more tasty. Remembering now, fleeting bits of horror movie dreams, soon to be totally forgotten. Thank heaven. Wish the bits of last night's remembrances would forget themselves as well. In time my memory will select against them, but for the moment they are all too vivid. Will go down to find the people still here. In messy heaps across the floor. I kick out of the sheets and land my feet on the icy linoleum. Where is my mat? I have a nice brown mat to stand up on in the mornings and now it's gone. Fallen prey to partying pirates. Everything in my life is someone's plunder. My stomach is manoeuvring fitfully like an airplane taking evasive action. Trying to get away from itself. I put on sweat shirt and jeans. This is the second-last day. Will I be left to mourn? Something tells me no. Anything, however, will be better than the St. Jude's Day Massacre.

The community will be fussing over the latest scandal. The story blown up some more. Probably arriving at some tale of how I was seen chasing Muriel who is Melanie across the barnyard with a rope over one shoulder and a broomstick in my hand. Stopped in the nick of time by Mr. Evans, who would have murdered me with his bare hands if the rest of the party hadn't stepped in. Smelling of nail polish, I was taken away by police for questioning.

Funny, I have always thought Muriel lower on the community's list of the condemned than I. Last night revealed the true calibration. Crowned King of the Perverts in something less than glory. My kingdom an unfortunate void. Everyone saying, no doubt, that I should be locked up. Not knowing that I already have been. Chains of cast iron would be pleasanter. Condemned to the dark gaol of the mind. Rat-like memories crawling around in me. Let's hear a chorus or two of "woe is me," in many-part harmony.

Must leave my room now and face the parents. Forgetless as elephants, they will confront me with fresh grievances. Slowly down the stairs. Ashes from careless cigarettes even here. Open the door on a panorama of what could only be described as pillage. The ashtrays are bulging and overspilled. Napkins scrunched and tossed. Sweets half-eaten and stepped on. Wading through the ashes, crumbs, and dropped utensils to the kitchen. Where Mother stands vacuuming. Looks at me briefly and back to the floor again. No acknowledgement given. Will be a small party at the airport at the present rate of loss in allies. Into the bathroom. Splash cold water on my face and feel dirty none the less. Brushing my teeth, refuel my toothbrush and brush some more, but part of the glue won't budge. My stomach hanging dead and unhappy. I brush my hair and an abnormal amount of it gives up its grip on my head. Stare at the dot of blond in the brush and pray. Would look very funny without hair. Have a funny-shaped head. A larger than normal bulge at the back. All these things considered and the morning's excretions accomplished, I feel very little improved. Want only to lie back down and wish this and many days to come completely away.

Back out to the kitchen. Mother still vacuuming. No mention of my breakfast. The best of traditions lie broken with the worst. I open the fridge and pick up an egg. I carry it to the stove. I set it down to look for a pan. It rolls off the stove and breaks in a wide splatter on Mother's freshly cleaned floor. She glowers. Saying nothing, she mops up the ill-fated egg and begins my breakfast. So goes the morning. As quiet as a mortuary. Activities alone giving voice.

"There was a phone call for you. The message is tacked up by the phone."

I look. It is from Athena.

"Tell Tyrone that there is going to be a small dinner party for me at my parents' house tonight. Tell him he is expected to attend. It's probably semi-formal so tell him to wear his brown sports jacket, light blue shirt, and brown tie. And the brown flares I gave him for his birthday. Tell him that if he wears those awful tan cords he's so fond of, I'll kill him. It's at eight sharp, so tell him to be fifteen minutes early."

Lightning has just struck twice. No respect for timing. Athena's parents also nurture a deep dislike for me. Had envisioned a nice young doctor for their only daughter. Got this farmer's son with less than impeccable manners and less than a toehold on the future. Conflicting totally with their grand design. Have trouble remembering which knife goes with the butter and have been known to eat the main course with my pie fork. And now my presence becomes a must. The need prompted by some strong rule of etiquette. Their unswaying sense of duty to the that-which-is-proper. They will all be there: aunts, uncles, beloved cousins. Giving the latest gowns and specially tailored suits their first breaths of high society air. Ignoring me exquisitely except for the odd, "And what do you do, young man?" All those who haven't had the pleasure of meeting me previously will be thinking I must be an artist, as all those who have already had the displeasure did. Was once severely reprimanded by Athena for telling her Uncle Harold, the oil tycoon, that I dabbled in eating, sleeping, and going for walks. I have now been schooled to reply that, although I haven't actually attended university for the past two and one half years, I have been doing private research toward a master's thesis and will probably return to university this year toward that end. In what? In Economics. I'm studying the finer points of Microeconomic Analysis. Am as yet undecided whether to go into business or to settle for an academic career. I feel, you see, that the neoclassical synthesis has become as obsolescent as its predecessors and is severely in need of wholesale revision. One must break economic theory back down to premises and rebuild it with a greater respect for the laws governing logic and philosophy.

And even at that, no one is convinced. More inclined to stare at my unpolished loafers and the roughness at the seams of my sports jacket and think me a useless dreamer. If a theory does not yield 30 per cent per annum, what good is it? A starving artist might even be better. For they are judged purposeful in a minor way. After all, if there were no starving artists, there would be no art exhibitions to go to. There would be no cultural causes, would there? It would hardly be respectable to dig in one's pocket for the promotion of better economic theory. There is the tradition of the token artist at every party to be thought of. Not their place really to part with the status quo and start having starving economists instead.

I can't go! To spend my second-last Canadian evening suffocating in the smoke of expensive cigars. This is no time for expatriating myself. Gobbling food purchased by American money. No time to salute those who would bulldoze Canada into the United States for processing.

What a peculiar loyalty this is! Loyalty to my father and his ferocious friends. And all those who suspect me of everything unwholesome. A strange sadness that bites me when I think of their ownership of the land ending six inches under the surface. And now, Athena expects me to come and drink to the health of her much celebrated Uncle Bobby whose job it is to exploit this law. Renting from the government the rights to what lies beneath. Waving fists full of company money, he shoves the surface owners around like pawns on a chessboard.

"It is in a way unfortunate, Mr. Jones, that our seismic reports reveal that your house sits upon the only truly feasible drilling location for the proposed M-12 well. Of course, you will be generously recompensed. What is that you say? Your family's homestead cabin first stood on this spot in 1895. We are, of course, truly sorry about all that. But, we must remind you that our company does have a lease on the mineral rights to this piece of property."

And so on, as so often happens. Wouldn't be such a miserable situation if the oil was to be of great use to Canadians. But not so. Drilled up and either processed here in American plants or shipped across the border to be processed there. Then we buy it all back in pretty cans and it's hard to believe it was ever ours. Now they want our water. I wonder if we could sell them Lake Erie. Would feel quite at home in America, I would think.

Can't really blame the Americans for everything; though we certainly try. Like putting a cat on your table and then reprimanding it when it eats. Still, not many cats will eat until they burst.

This moral soliloquy is an awful lot to have on my sleepy mind so early in the day. Should do the traditionally Canadian thing and blot it out of my thoughts.

Only the farmers do not shy away from it all. There are few plums on the oil industry's tree to pacify them. Some turn their thoughts away. When their son perhaps becomes a junior operator at a plant and they decide his future is more important than theirs. But for most, the plants offer little except polluted air and water. And their traditionally generous recompense for carving your land into jagged pieces.

Some who farmed for reasons other than preference have grown to enjoy it. Have found farming the oil companies more lucrative and enjoyable than farming their land. All these cases admitted. But not for most. Not for Father, who derives so little joy now from farming his dismembered plots.

How incredibly sad I am today! All these people who would go to such great lengths to keep me away from their societies. Making me wonder if I'll ever fit in anywhere. Somewhere among the slots that people fit in, I stand so alone. Banging on only this door for admittance. I look at Mother and her look says, "No, Tyrone. Not even here." This, my only vestige of a home being quickly barred.

Can I be held responsible for what I turned out like? If I had had great mechanical abilities and had overcome my fear of horses enough to look the part of a cowboy, would I still be facing this irreversible expulsion? No. It's all because I was born a coward.

All the poor cowards in this world. We suffer from one of the few unsympathized-with maladies. No one is accused and reprimanded for having cancer, or being a schizophrenic, or having poor vision. Even homosexuality and drug abuse are viewed with greater tolerance. But who pats the coward on the back and says, "That's all right, friend"? Who says, "You poor dear"? Who else can complain of being the object of universal contempt?

No matter what quantity of boundless sympathy I pour into the cause of Canada, I will never be accepted. Not that acceptance is my goal. But, it would be a welcome fringe benefit.

Should forget about all this and get to the matters at hand. Accept my fate as an ever-lonely crusader and forge on.

"Your father and I are very unhappy with you, Tyrone." Mother is speaking in measured syllables. She saves this mode of speech for women's club meetings and grave reprimands. To convey that she has dignity in such sordid situations.

"Yes, I know."

"We feel that you deliberately set out to embarrass us in front of our friends. It is something we are not likely to forget."

"Mother, I didn't deliberately set out to do anything. I'm not going to make a big speech about my innocence. I am sorry for being indiscreet, but I'm not going to apologize for telling the truth."

"Some truth! It wasn't even St. Jude's Day."

"Oh, Jesus!"

"And I think you've used the Lord's name in vain quite enough. I don't want to hear any more of your dirty-mouthed profanity."

"Count your lucky stars then, Mother, because after 2:30 PM on Monday, you won't have to hear my voice at all."

"I must admit that you've put an awful strain on the regret your father and I will feel over seeing you leave."

"In plain English, you won't give a damn. And you don't need to feel that you have to come to the airport either."

I stomp to the phone and dial Athena. The phone rings and rings. I slam the receiver down. Will be difficult to sustain this angry courage until Athena returns. Will need it to convey my determination not to attend her parents' party. I ring again. Let it buzz on and on. Finally Athena announces a breathless hello.

"I'm not coming."

"What?"

"I can't come."

"Why?"

"Because I don't want to."

"What now, Tyrone?"

"I have just been through several rotten things and would prefer not to come."

"Oh god, Tyrone! My parents are expecting you. They'll be insulted as hell if you don't turn up."

"Your parents hate me and so do all the rest of your relatives that I have met. They really won't care."

"That's all in your head, Tyrone. You're always feeling persecuted. There's not one good reason why you can't come."

"Don't nag me, Athena."

"I'm not nagging you! I don't nag! You can go ahead and vegetate out there if you like. Feel persecuted as you bloody well like. I don't care if you insult me and my parents and the rest of the family and accuse them of things they don't do. Call me a nag all you want!"

"I'll pick you up at eight."

"That's too late! You'll have to be here at seven-thirty."

THE WORLD is foul with rationality. This I conclude as I drive toward Athena's city. No one will accept an emotional reason as a good enough reason for anything. Said I didn't want to come because I feel persecuted by her relatives. Not good enough. It would have had to be something sensible like vomiting sick. Something concrete would have had to be standing in my way. "Wild horses couldn't hold me back" goes from platitude to anachronism in one jump as swift as progress. Wild horses holding you back becomes one of few admissible excuses rather than clever hyperbole. I am driving twenty miles an hour below the speed limit and a steady stream of more eager drivers floods by. If this trip took the rest of my life to complete, it might in many ways be a pleasanter end. For I look into the future and see only desert on all my life's horizons.

Athena, that one and only flower that I deliver water and nutrients to so faithfully. And she threatens to wilt and die from my life. Fearful thoughts. A life without her would be abject misery. I arrive at that by simple subtraction. Life with her being the second most abject of miseries.

The darkness drops as discernibly as a fog and I wonder will the sun ever rise again. I wouldn't blame it if it decided not to. Not even an object of worship any more. Expected to cross the sky without payment or praise. I sympathize and identify. For I am expected to rise each day and no one salutes me for the effort either. No one marks it as praiseworthy or courageous, even though by getting up I increase the chance of accident a hundredfold. And now I am expected to go to Athena's family get-together. To absorb the silent abuses unpaid. A dartboard for all their money-corrupted aggressions. I come free with each daughter. Didn't even have to send coupons or boxtops. Few things like me in this world. The item you are not obliged to either pay for or appreciate. Who would have thought it possible?

11: The Strength of Tradition

I KNOCK on the door. No answer. Perhaps Athena decided to go without me. I pound once more. Windows rattle. Finally the door flies open. Athena before me in a state of half dress. In a towel, to be precise.

"Hi, sweetie. You must be still in a filthy mood. You almost pounded the door down."

She kisses my cheek and kicks the door shut behind me. Lets the towel drop. Oh shit!

"I just had a very nice bath and let's see, it's seven-thirty on the nose. So, you're early and I'm late."

"Let's make love."

"Silly you. Of course we can't. We'd be late for the party."

"Might miss it altogether."

"You'd like that, wouldn't you?"

Athena vanishes into her room leaving me suspended in my desire. Could go in and attack her. She has so little respect for my animalism. Doesn't take it very seriously. Thinks that free love and non-embarrassment about sexual matters are the same as being mildly disinterested. To truly be casual about sex, you must be slightly bored. In that case, bring back the bodice. Swath them back up in miles of cloth. So it will be all the more suspenseful to dig through. Bring back the taboos and the shotgun weddings. To pump the excitement back into the whole business. I am ever a skeptic in these matters of progress. For freedom is such an unadventuresome business. Not that I crave very much adventure. Good advertisement for my theory. That even someone as cowardly as I cannot find excitement enough in this world.

Athena returns suddenly gowned. Floor-length dress. Dangling earrings. Wide sash pinching her in below her bust.

I stare at her proudly, forgetting what a shabby image I make beside her.

"Who says the female can't dress quickly?"

"And expertly."

"The voice of chivalry itself, aren't you?"

I walk up and give her a long kiss. She plucks a handkerchief out from nowhere and wipes lipstick off me. Steps back and critically examines me.

"Shoes unpolished, threadbare sports jacket, tie knot too small, tie tack off centre, collar up, shirt tucked in unevenly, cigarette ashes on your pants. Tyrone, what am I going to do with you?"

"Accept me."

"I haven't got much choice, have I?"

"I hope not." She pulls me here and flattens me there and dusts me all over. And then grimaces that the net result isn't much better. She leads me out and into my truck.

The lights of this small city whiz by. Little activity even on this, a Saturday night.

"What was overtime like?"

"A piece of cake. I didn't do anything except take a bit of dictation. And I typed a couple of letters. Three hours at time-and-a-half for that. I can't for the life of me understand why he kept me over at all."

"I can."

"Oh, can you? Why for instance?"

"He probably had naughty plans."

"What? Ha. Ha. That's funny, Tyrone. If you could only see Mr. Forbes you'd know how funny that is. He's about a hundred. He shakes and everything."

"Well, he probably had you work over so he could look at you all night."

"God, you're suspicious, Tyrone. You must think everyone in the world is after my body or something."

"Most everyone who's seen it probably is."

"You're doing great things for my ego, but I really doubt it."

I pull into the Tills' drive. Take my place around the asphalt circle in front of their mansion. Jaguars, Lincolns, Cadillacs; and now, one old red farm truck with bits of hay clinging to the corners of its box. And I will now go inside to be just as well-suited to the company there.

The Tills and their kind are worse in this particular city than they would be anywhere else. When they get together, they soak one another in royal affectation. I think I have an inkling of why Brookside has no clubs, no high-class restaurants. In short, no place for the very rich to go and be recognized as the very rich. The Tills and their kind are a tiny minority and their occasional spreading of wealth couldn't keep any plush establishment in business. So the poor dears suffer ignominy. What use is great wealth if there is no outlet for it? What use is being rich if you are in no position to see the envy in the public eye?

They, of course, would live elsewhere if they could. Probably in Calgary where prosperity is abundant enough to be flauntable. But those to whom they kneel and pay homage have planted them here and here they stay. Ha. Ha. How that pleases me as I climb the stone steps between sculpted beasts. They flock together like frightened children. Putting on what they hope are real airs. Commenting on the quality of the wine although they probably don't have a clue. No one reprimands anyone. Too unsure of what is presently correct. The Avant Garde: an object of desire and fear. Athena enters and is greeted by her tiptoeing mother. So weighed down with bangles, I'm surprised she can walk. A little sticky-mouthed peck on the cheek for Athena. Unsurprisingly, I am not being noticed. Moustachioed Daddy staggers out brandishing his girth. Rosy-cheeked as a baby and inflated as a toad, he too applies lips to Athena.

"Oh, and here's Tyrone. How are you, dear?"

She grabs my hand. It dangles in her shaking clutch.

"And how are you, Mrs. Till?"

"Splendid, Tyrone. I had a little touch of flu last week but lovely Dr. Stoneman fixed me right up."

"That's good, Mrs. Till. I'm glad you're feeling better."

"Look Simon, Tyrone's here."

Simon looks suddenly ill but a wax smile finally assembles itself. He extends his hand and I shake the soft, pudgy thing. Like picking up a handful of worms.

"Good to see you, Tyrone. Did you have a good trip?"

"Very good, thanks. Yes, it was very good."

We are delivered into the living room and there is a lot of wheezing and sighing. Everyone lining up to kiss Athena. While I shake an uninteresting assortment of hands. Little bits of my flesh being ripped out by great, gaudy dinner rings. Should start slipping them off these fingers while I smile idiotically into the painted faces. Could make a sizable haul. Might find out they are all just glass. More affectation.

All these women are so bloodless. Just little wax apparatuses after they pop out of the hairdressers and face fabricators for the millionth time.

All the men are flabby. Pink from short wind and lack of sun. Most with closely cropped moustaches. Their six wisps of remaining head hair carefully set into place twice a week at the men's salon. Great drooping asses from continuous sitting. But now, of course, they stand. One of their rules that you stand while sipping your drink and munching hors d'oeuvres. And I play along with everything. Bowing and grinning and saying, "No, I am not an artist but an economist," and so on.

"Did you see the lovely exhibition of pastels by that new artist, what's his name? Well it's slipped my mind, isn't that funny? But they are marvellous, dear."

"I guess I'm just not with it but Updike's new book is far too obscene for my tastes. Do you think I'm not with it, dear?"

"Well, dear, if you're not, I'm not either because I find so much of the new art offensive to my sense of taste. What do you think, Tyrone?"

"Oh yes, I couldn't agree more."

"Did you see that film at the cinema this week? It was positively disgusting. I could hardly watch it."

"The film censors are going from one extreme to another, I think. What do you think, Tyrone?"

"I couldn't agree more."

The sight of bare bums makes me gag. Yes, Mrs. Stoneman, yes. But I will drink very conservatively. Eat as daintily as my ignorance allows, and keep all the things I wish I could say safely tucked in my mind. All for Athena. Yes, the conservation laws are silly. Yes, the Americans should be allowed to exploit us. Since we don't seem to have the sense to exploit ourselves. Yes, its horrible that the hunting season is so short and that you are restricted to murdering only one elk per year. Yes, it's a shame that you went camping last August and couldn't even build a fire. Yes, I can just imagine how disappointed your children were. That they didn't have a chance to watch a forest burn down. Oh, I agree. Something should be done about it all. No one should have the right to put a leash on you. You should be allowed to pig up the world.

"Did you hear the one about the Ukrainian who walks into the doctor's office with a pig on his head."

"No, Mr. Barnsley, I didn't."

"Well, the doctor says, 'What can I do for you, sir?' And the pig answers, 'I was wondering if you could cut this ugly growth off my ass.' Ha. Ha."

"Ha. Ha. Funny I haven't heard that one. My Ukrainian granny will love it."

As Mr. Barnsley gets pinker, I think, oops. But that's only one slip all night. An admirable performance, I think.

Walking along with a goblet of champagne. I haven't seen Athena in ages. Another rule of etiquette under the sub-heading of: Being a Good Mixer. You bring your wife or whomever, dispense with her, and only start looking for her again when it's time to leave. Find her in some funny places, I would imagine. I find Athena sitting across a coffee table from celebrated Uncle Bobby in the dimly lit sunken living room. They are alone. Bobby speaking earnestly. Athena staring down into her lap. Looking much the part of a little girl being lectured for doing something shameful. I approach slowly, hoping to catch an earful before I'm noticed.

"I'm sure he's a fine person in his way but . . ."

Athena sees me. "Ah, here's Tyrone. Where've you been, honey?"

"Just mingling. Hello, Mr. Till."

Mr. Till nods, looking a little embarrassed. He picks up his glass.

"Well, I'll leave you two lovebirds alone." With a much-practised wink, Bobby is gone.

"What was all that about?"

"Oh nothing much. Just a lot of advice. You know how Uncle Bobby is." Athena looks sad. A bit bedraggled in all her finery.

"It was about me, wasn't it?"

"There you go again, always . . ."

"Oh, come on! I overheard. I just want to know what he said, and more importantly, what you think about what he said."

Do I really, I think, surprised at myself.

"Oh, Tyrone, I don't know what to think about it all. I just wish they all liked you more. He was being quite polite. He just said he didn't think you were my type and that I was bound to find that out over in Europe and that I should be emotionally prepared for the worst."

Athena is going to cry, I think. Since women seem to be crying continuously, you would think that the makers of cosmetics would create their products to withstand it. Those ugly black smears certainly take the charm out of female grief.

"What do you think? You're obviously not certain that he's wrong."

"Sit over here." I move over and plant myself at Athena's side on the narrow couch. She leans her head on my shoulder. "I really don't know, Tyrone. I told him he was wrong and all that, but I really don't know you very well. You always seem to be keeping so much from me. It's not the way Uncle Bobby thinks it is. He probably thinks you're a weirdo and that you're never going to amount to much and all that. But even if that's true, I don't mind. It's all part of you. And since that's the part of you I know, it's also the part of you I like. It's all the stuff I don't know that scares me."

"Maybe we shouldn't go." Hope tingles through me. Those deadened cells in charge of my enthusiasm wriggle with life once more.

"No, Tyrone. That isn't the problem. I'm just scared of you and all your dark sides. The setting isn't really important. If the situation in Europe draws out the problems, maybe it's for the better."

My heart plummets down a familiar hole. "Whatever you think."

The European situation threatens to stamp out all my sides, light and dark. We sit here in this suburb of the party. Loaded with our various types of remorse. We are as quiet and pathetic as a soft sigh. Finally Athena sits up, hankys off her makeup, and, staring in her small mirror, rebuilds it again.

"You're not enjoying yourself, are you?"

"No."

"I can't blame you, I guess. They're my relatives and friends of my family and I have a hard time coping with them all sometimes. You haven't been insulting them, have you?"

"No. My manners have been quite good considering my upbringing."

"I don't think it's that that they mind."

"If I was a farmer's son who was aspiring to be a doctor, they might forget about my humble beginnings, eh?"

"Let's not talk about it. It's not important to me, really. Well, it is important; but, it isn't vital or anything that they like you."

"Good to hear it."

"Do you mind if we go back and mingle some more? I warn you, the teary toasts are yet to come."

"Oh. I'll limber up my tear ducts then."

Athena smiles and squeezes my arm. Then gone. I remain for a moment lighting a cigarette. Wondering if it's necessary that Athena should ever know all of me. Would wish it different. For when she knows me completely, Uncle Bobby's prediction must come true. Wouldn't be like my daring Athena to put up with a coward.

12: Travelling on a Limited Budget

I WANDER back into the overgrown ballroom. Its immense chandelier hanging wreathed in smoke. Paintings from local exhibitions hung here and there. A bust of George Washington atop a pillar in the corner. Beside it, a rubber tree growing from a gold-embroidered pot. To my mind a conglomeration of junk in the worse of taste. Assembled over time on the basis of where there was room, the embellishments are staggered at regular intervals along the wall. I glance to the side to find Athena's father rocking on his heels.

"Looks like you need a drink, my boy." He waves a waiter over and sticks a glass in my hand. "I'd like to have a talk with you, Tyrone. Have you got a minute?" I nod. He slaps a hand on my shoulder and leads me to the living room. "I just thought, since you'll be seeing the most of my daughter for the next few months, I ought to have a word with you." He motions me to a chair and pulls his close.

"You and Athena aren't serious, are you?"

"We're not planning immediate marriage, if that's what you mean."

"That's good to hear. Although you make a fine couple, I don't think either of you are prepared to accept that kind of responsibility . . . There's something else bothering me, Tyrone. I just hope that you understand that Athena is used to a certain level of comfort which I don't imagine you can afford. I wouldn't want to think that you are going to be encouraging Athena to sleep rough, so to speak, while you're in Europe – to meet your budget I mean." I can stand this no longer.

"Mr. Till, there are a few things I'd like to say to you as well. First, I intend on returning your daughter to you single and intact. And second, I have slightly more money to spend on this trip than you have given Athena." In my mind I continue: third, you are a bloody hypocrite, an ignorant expatriate, a corporate puppet. I get up and walk away wishing I hadn't said anything. Sleep rough, though! How is a person to put up with that particular turd? Adrenaline is raging through me. Mr. Till calls me back. I ignore him at first but finally return.

"I see I have insulted you, Tyrone. My apologies." I nod. "Still you must understand my concern. Athena is our only child."

"Would you be honest with me for a moment, Mr. Till?"

"Why certainly. I am always honest with you." You incredibly brazen liar.

"Did you put your brother up to trying to convince Athena not to go to Europe with me?" He looks shocked.

"Certainly not."

"Then he was acting on his own initiative?"

"I don't know what you're talking about."

"Well, since I know that you do, I just want to let you know that he botched it."

"Tyrone, I did not . . ."

"He put way too much emphasis on how rotten I am and not nearly enough emphasis on how rotten Europe could be with me."

"This is preposterous!"

"I thought people in your line of business would be cleverer about a thing like that. You know, using human nature to club people into line. Making them think that what you want them to do is in their best interests."

"I don't have to sit here and listen . . ."

"I'm just curious whether it was your idea or whether Bobby just screwed it up. Or did you pour your stupidities together to come up with such a lousy plan?"

I am talking in a flat monotone. Solidly badgering Athena's dearest father. Making him squirm beautifully. He stands up and yells, "Enough!"

The exertion of it has caused him to sweat slightly and one clump of his hair has fallen in front of his face. Quite a lot of attention is now focused on us. His shout would have broken crystal. Several faces are bunched at the door. Athena's mother, looking worried, ploughs to the front of the crowd.

"Is anything wrong, Simon?"

"No, Deirdre, no. I was just telling Tyrone a story. I guess I got carried away. Sorry if I have caused a disturbance."

The people filter away again. Disappointed. Hoping there would be a twenty-four-karat scene. As soon as they are gone, he reseats himself and, pushing his face up into mine, he says, "I don't want you to see my daughter again. Now leave my house."

A new plan is forging.

"I would be very pleased to leave your house. Mr. Till. But, you might have trouble convincing Athena that she doesn't want to see me again. But, feel free to try. You only have tomorrow to stop her from going with me. Might be quite a chore. Think you can do it?"

"Don't bet against it, kid. You've locked horns with more than you can handle this time. Now get out."

I walk away, rubbing my hands in delight. You never know when Fate's going to deal you a good card. Out of all this misery has come almost surefire success. It is all so simple. Tonight or at latest tomorrow, Athena's father will put his foot down. I will get a phone call from Athena telling me how everything's gone wrong and her father won't allow her to go. Threatening to cut her out of his will or something classic like that. I will say, that's too bad, but not the end of the world. I, of course, won't leave without you, Athena. No. No. I don't mind. It's just one of those things I'll have to forego. Maybe some other day we can do it. (Ha. Ha.)

There will be a dramatic time when Athena and I carry on our affair in secrecy. Our relationship will acquire strength in surmounting the interference. All will be glorious and most important, it will be glorious right here. Everyone will be full of sympathy and Athena's father will bear all the weight of blame. Splendid day. I find Athena in the conversational clutches of another relative. Aunt Mildred, I think.

"Excuse me, Mrs. Barnsley. Could I borrow Athena for about half a minute. I'll return her to you shortly."

"No, that's fine."

I drag Athena a bit away.

"I have to leave."

"What now, Tyrone? You promised not to be difficult."

"Your father and I had an argument. I'm sorry it happened, but it was inevitable. He has invited me to leave."

"Oh no, Tyrone! What a crappy evening! How did it happen?"

"He thinks that I'm going to have you 'sleeping rough' in Europe. I presume that means under trees, or on park benches, or with me."

"Oh god! I'll get my coat."

"No. You can't go. Just say I have a headache. If you leave, there'll be a hell of a row."

"I guess you're right. I'll fetch your coat."

As Athena carts my coat back, various people ask where I am going. She explains my headache. They all think, he doesn't appear to be the sort who would have any stamina. Mrs. Till rushes up.

"Are you leaving, Tyrone?"

"Yes, Mrs. Till. I have a headache. I guess I just don't have the stamina to celebrate two nights in succession. Sorry I have to leave your lovely party. It won't cause any inconvenience, will it?"

"Well, of course we're sorry to see you go. But if you don't feel up to it, we shall certainly not expect you to stay."

"Thank you, Mrs. Till. Here's Athena with my coat." I climb into it and thank everyone copiously. Wave bye-bye to the crowd.

"Where's Simon?"

"Oh, don't disturb him, Mrs. Till. Just thank him for me for the wonderful time."

I leave. Athena walks with me.

"Hell, I forgot you haven't got your car."

"It doesn't matter. If you're going home I'll just stay here. I wish this had turned out better. You didn't provoke Father, did you?"

"Well, he didn't provoke himself."

"You started it then."

"No, he definitely started it."

"Oh, what difference does it make anyway?"

I shrug. "Beats me. Look, Athena, don't worry. This'll all blow over eventually."

We neck around at my truck door for maybe an hour. Athena would feel very nice in bed tonight. Warm and sad like romance should be. But must exercise a certain restraint tonight. So that such nights can continue long into the winter. My plan will go off at optimum efficiency with Athena staying here tonight. Must stop this rubbing of heated bodies. View the greater goal. My body trying to confuse the issue considerably. Has its own idea as to what qualifies as the greater goal.

"Oh, Tyrone. I want to make love to you tonight. Do you think that everyone and everything will ever get out of our way long enough so that we can do as we please?"

"Some day." I lie. "Must go now, before we make an exhibition of ourselves under your father's cherished maple tree. Would be kind of a fitting farewell to Canada though, don't you think?"

"I think I lost you somewhere."

"Making love under a maple tree. I just thought it would be fitting."

"I guess so."

Athena doesn't follow me. But that is all right. To understand me fully, she would have to know me fully; and I, of course, do not want that. How is she to envision what I now envision – us lying naked on this frosty evening blanketed in maple leaves. Like being buried at sea wrapped in a flag.

I board my truck. Start it and roar the engine. Mouth affections to Athena. See you Monday morning. Confident that I won't. Waving as I pull away from these wealthy autos. Athena blows kisses.

Off down the aisles of street lights. Athena left standing on the asphalt. Suddenly remembering that it is cold, she will shiver and wrap arms around herself. Go back into the so-restrained frolic. Someone will get up to do the foxtrot to an old seventy-eight as the evening ebbs.

Am I cruel to put Athena through the now inevitable torture of a shouting argument with her father? So often I wind these clocks and am far, far away as their tick carves notches in the lives of others. I think it will be the best thing for Athena in the long run. Knowing full well that this is bullshit. Athena would be very much better off with a full-futured doctor. Who would work hard and rise high and never feel the slightest urge to put his initials on the ice cream in a grocery store bucket.

I can't help wanting her for my own, though. I would even marry her if she wished. A small pain compared to what I've already suffered to keep her. But still I wonder, have I any right to keep my foot in her life's door? Butting so eagerly into her future? Silly question, really. Selfishness, I presume, knows no right or wrong. Or at least bravely overlooks these classifications. Desire obliterates the conscience. And so it goes with my Athena. I can say I have no right to keep her, but what matter, when I ruthlessly struggle for her anyway. Much rather feel guilty than lonely.

And still there is a little bit of soothing ointment for my conscience. I am not greedy in the boundless sense of American imperialism. I am only small-time greedy. Want only one other creature to share my failings willingly. And want that creature to be Athena. That's the world I wish for.

13: Know Your History

SUNDAY. So much like a million Sundays. Mother in her chair furiously knitting something which reaches ever-closer to the floor. In a few years, it will be inching its way into the kitchen. Father sits in my spot on the couch reading his newspaper. Grunting disapprovingly every few sentences. A dozen clocks tick.

Because Father is in my spot, I have to sit in the foreign armchair. A spring in its middle, acquiring strength with age, is butting obtrusively at my ass. May yet win its war with the cover fabric and propel me whooping into the air. A solo note of excitement to this barely humming Sunday.

There is no distraction, save the spring, to keep me from my case of nerves. Athena has not phoned. My foolproof plan has somehow flopped.

I lift my guitar from behind the chair. Where Mother always hides it. And strum all the minor chords I know. In many original variations. Hoping to discover a particularly miserable one.

"Sing, Tyrone."

"I can't sing, Mother."

"Oh, you can too, I've heard you when you didn't know I was listening."

Stage-struck. Mother is smiling: an attempt at reconciliation. "All right."

I start picking out the simple notes of a song by Leonard Cohen. Very deliberately chosen. For its soothing effect. I will apply it like salve to all my wounds.

"It's called 'Winter Lady.'"

I sing the small number of verses. Which lull me like a hypnotist's words. Granting me a convincing absolution. Slips a feather wedge between each word and its trailing guilt. I imagine it ending in a soft sigh. Leaving me caught in dreams of strange and eerie farewells.

"Did you have to sing a dirty song?"

"What."

"Just because your mother asked politely for you to sing a song, you had to go and sing a dirty one. Didn't you?"

"I didn't think it was dirty, Tom."

"It sure as hell was and he sang it on purpose."

I get up. Toss my guitar onto the couch and walk out into the porch. I pull on my old parka, heavy socks, and gumboots. And launch into the ice-cold sunshine. I look around for Plato, that uncritical friend. I call him, but he does not come. Must be out sniffing after long-gone rabbits. As a last hope, I glance into his doghouse. And there he is, wrapped round himself. Looking cold and sleepy. I climb into his smelly little room. He crawls up on me and licks my face. I let him. He tires of the taste of me and sprawls his front quarters across my crossed legs. I finger his ears so soft and expensive-feeling. "Plato, the world is an unfit mother. But we're stuck with her, aren't we?"

Taking his cue from the misery in my voice, Plato moans.

"Too bad people aren't as willing to do that as you, Plato. Then I wouldn't mind so much." And there we stay for a long time. Plato drifts off to sleep and leaves me staring at his walls. Now and again, he jerks in reaction to his dog dreams. Now he has jerked so hard he has awakened himself. What did you dream, Plato? In our dreams, we all have giant fears, don't we? No one can claim a life without nightmares. Sleep renders us all equal in our cowardice. Too bad no one thinks of the time they woke up sweating and terrified when they're in the process of judging one such as me. It's just a simple reaction, isn't it, Plato? When you dream of a stronger foe, you jump with fear. As simple as two plus two. I'm just an unfortunate case of true vision. I can't stunt the size of my foes in daytime or inflate the size of me. I see them as they are. Cyclops. Giants.

I am so puny in relation.

I am the one that the weakling at the beach comes looking for after his humiliation at the feet of the sand-kicking bully. Egos feed on me. I will run from anything. But, I was laughed at when I said there was a social need for cowards. Told my sociology class that we should be paid by the hour to absorb society's shit and abuse. Shallow bastards didn't understand.

A humbug on social workers! Think they all have a message for humanity. Would swear up and down that their helping hands are extended everywhere. Yet, who sponsors "Take a Coward Out For Dinner Week"? No one! The mercy is all dispensed to the hungry, the sick, the crazy, and the crippled. And there is none left over for me. Even you, Plato, are better off. There is the SPCA and the Dog Lovers' Club for you to look up in times of need. But where can I go? Not even home.

When my trials have finally driven me mad, hordes of social workers will rush to take hold of my shaking hands. And won't they all feel holy then? To have overcome their revulsion for this putrid madman. For having the pluck to lead me to the madhouse.

They think that sainthood is within their easy grasp. Only three years of being sprayed with academic paint and you pop out feeling just like Florence Nightingale. Total absolution given for all prior sins. One good that you do erases all bad that you did before. The day you pushed little brother off the roof and he broke his arm and leg: all forgiven when you cart me off to be lobotomized.

Unfair that they should be allowed to feel sanctimonious and sinless. While I am accused of everything. Just a matter of time until I am blamed for winter.

Mother yells to Plato that his dinner is ready and he scrambles over me to go and get it. I must leave now too. Quickly. As long as Plato is here, he is the obvious choice of any flea looking for a home. In his absence, it's any port in a storm. I hustle after him. Mother sees me.

"What were you doing in there?"

"Plato and I were discussing his Theory of Forms."

I walk toward the house and Mother waits, holding the scraped-out potato bowl and spoon. Plato is oblivious to all but what lies in his dish.

"I'm sorry about that business about the song. I thought it was very nice."

"Thank you."

"And don't think too harshly of your father. The type of life we lead here maybe makes Tom a bit narrow. But that can't be helped. You have to be willing to bend a little because your father isn't likely to. It's too late in his life now."

"Narrow? How can you say that Father's narrow? He eats well, sleeps well, farms well, drinks well, belches expertly, and plays great poker from what I've been told. Father's not narrow."

"Don't be so sarcastic."

"I don't want Father to be a swinger. If he smoked marijuana and sang rhythm and blues while he drove his tractor, I wouldn't get along with him any better. All I want from Father is that he think back a little. Surely to god his life hasn't always been tractors and grain quotas. That song was about being young and wanting things that you want because you're young. I hate to think what a lousy place Father's mind must be if he thinks that's dirty."

Mother looks very sad now, I think I have opened old wounds. "Tyrone, I don't think you know very much about your father. The truth is that his life has been mostly tractors and grain quotas. When all the other boys were going off to war, your father was exempted because he had to take care of the farm. His father died during the war, you see. And before that, the Depression kept him home. He couldn't have made a living if he had started drifting. Your father never really had a chance to be young. He was even very businesslike about marrying me, I'm afraid. It wasn't one of those relationships where you spend a lot of time walking under the stars. Grain quotas had a lot to do with it, actually. Your father decided he could afford a wife one winter, so we got married. Do you see now why he understands you so little?"

"I'm sorry."

"Oh, I'm not complaining. Tom's a very good man. He's always treated me like gold. You see, Tyrone, our generation never scolds over what it didn't get. We're happy that we got anything at all."

After Mother goes back inside, I spend a lot of time sitting on the verandah rail. In a few sentences, she has summed up why I have not murdered Father in his bed. It is different to be narrow-minded from choice than to be narrow-minded from lack of choice. If Father had, from myriad possible ideologies, picked his out, I would loathe him. But, I don't suppose he can be blamed for the history that shaped him.

But Mother falls short in her generalization too. Only a small segment of her generation is as satisfied as she claims it all to be. Too many people benefited from wartime and other sufferings and they will never be satisfied. No one can argue with me that the American imperialist, who has now come to own one-quarter of the world, isn't setting his sights on half.

14: The Moment of Truth

"I DON'T know why she puts up with you in the first bloody place. Men must be damned scarce when a poor excuse like you can have such a nice one."

"Would you mind not raving any more. I'm starting to get a headache."

"You poor little dear. Maybe if you try your charm out on your mother, she'll rub your temples for you."

"Oh Jesus!"

"I'm telling you, kid, if you were at all smart, you'd've married Athena as soon as you had the chance. It would be bloody worse luck for her life, but she's the only quality woman there's ever going to be in yours!"

"Athena doesn't even want to get married."

"Can't blame her for that."

"Not just me. She doesn't want to marry anyone."

"I still can't blame her. If she thinks you're the best she can get, of course she wouldn't want to marry anyone."

"Oh god! Mother! Are you sure Athena didn't call?"

"Of course I'm sure, Tyrone. I've been in all day."

What's going on out there at the Till estates? I hope her father didn't murder her in rage. But what if she just silently acquiesced? Decided I wasn't much after all and is just going to quietly drop out of my life? I'll drown myself! I wonder where I could buy a cheap millstone.

I can't stand it any longer. I must know what has gone wrong. It's now eight o'clock. Enough time has elapsed for a nuclear war. Modern family disagreements don't take an entire day. Father, who hates the cat as much as I do, has let him into the house to torture me. It beelines for me and starts sharpening its claws in my leg. Nice pussycat. Should get you a part in the movies. Saw one recently where a big fat pussycat just like you gets hung on a light cord. I don't really mean that, pussycat. (In case you're telepathic.) It's just that I am destroyed by worry and don't like your claws in my leg. Why don't you be a nice pussycat and go out and hunt a poisoned mouse?

I cannot wait any longer! I feel out the numbers. The operator comes on, "Your number, please."

"Four-three-three-two-nine-five-nine."

"Pardon me. There is some interference on the line."

"Four as in four times four makes sixteen; three as in three blind mice; three again as in Holy Trinity; two as in bisexual; nine as in a baseball game; five as in a basketball game; and another nine, this time as in six plus three blind mice."

"I have enough trouble on this job without people making nuisance calls! That number you've given me has way too many digits. If I had any idea who you are, I'd have you prosecuted!" Bang!

I think I have just joined Uncle Alfred in mono-hearing. I dial again. Same operator. Life is too short. "Four-three-three-two-nine-five-nine."

"Are you the guy who just called?"

"No, but if you'd like to prosecute him, his name is Simon Till." Bang!

How am I going to get by this hurdle? I think I am going crazier by the minute. Bring on the bleeding hearts. The ones with the strait jackets hidden behind their backs. Enticing me with oats. I will munch while they bridle me and coo, "Nice Tyrone." Just one question before I am lobotomized. What went on behind the locked doors of Till Mansion on that ever-blacker-looking Sunday?

I ring again. New operator. No interference. No complications. I hear the Tills' expensive phone which does not ring but plays bagpipes. Who will answer? It is Mrs. Till. Gracie for short.

"Can I speak to Athena, please?"

"I don't know if I should let you. Whatever possessed you to speak to Simon the way that you did?"

"Well, Mrs. Till, sometimes I just feel sort of like a trumpet; and then, I just can't help playing 'Taps' on myself. If you know what I mean."

"I must say I didn't expect all this sort of thing from you, Tyrone. It's a good thing we found out about you before you absconded with our daughter. I hate to think what you would have done to her in Europe."

"Why don't you let her tell me all these things herself? Quite candidly, Gracie, you've been acting a little strange these past weeks and I'm afraid you've been imagining things again."

"I'm going to hang up."

"You could be hearing a lot of bagpipes tonight," I hear shouting in the background. Superb anarchy! The phone is now being fought over. I hear Athena's voice telling her mother to back off or she's going to club her with the receiver.

"Hello, Tyrone! I can't talk now! All hell is breaking loose! It's awful! I'll phone later!" Bang!

I'm going quite deaf in that ear. Must learn to switch from side to side.

I feel a grin stretching all over my face. Athena is obviously remaining faithful. She will continue to maintain that inner fortification, even as the outer walls fall. The trip to Europe will be the first thing to crumble into ruin.

"Were you saying all those terrible things to Athena?"

"It's just a little joke we have between us, Mother. All in good fun. See. See me grin." Mother sees me grin.

"You sounded pretty serious to me."

"The more serious the better. It's no fun having a joke if it sounds like a joke, is it?" Mother leaves me grinning. Just about always leaves when she has some fresh reason for thinking I'm nuts. She puts these parts of me out of sight in hopes that she can stamp them out of mind.

What a treat today has been. After all these tortured weeks with nothing to look forward to but more black despair and high odds in favour of early death. Then, a day such as today, so rare in life, when Fate's evil plan is found out and scuppered. I will take this day off from whatever I have to do from now on, and celebrate it with votive lamps and private masses. Drink healths to it. Give it presents. For I am almost certain to live longer now.

As the terror is officially past and I sit smugly successful, I think I'll coldly analyse it all. Become paternal with myself and say: "Good has come of this, Tyrone." For instance, whither departed is your terror of wind? Although you are still most definitely a coward, your fears have diminished, become less unwieldy, a tidier cross to bear. You haven't even been conscious of how the wind has blown in the past week. You've almost been drawn to it, in fact, as part of the all which is Canada. And that is another fear that has shrivelled. That of Canada itself. Your eye in the hurricane has yawned. So large that its borders are now those of the nation. You would still not exactly glory in a journey to Nova Scotia, but you wouldn't sweat blood in preparation either. Home is an expanded term. You, Tyrone, are aspiring to normalcy. (Theoretical normalcy, of course. Canadians not being the sort to weep over distant cataclysm within what is officially nicknamed Canada.)

"What are you grinning so idiotically about?"

"Father, why do you hate me?" Father flushes red with embarrassment. Likes his life to be a distant thing. Feels naked and childish, stooping to speak of his emotions. "I mean it. Two weeks ago, you were satisfied to be embarrassed that I was your son. Then, suddenly, you began to hate me. Why?"

I think Father is actually going to face up to this confrontation. "Since, for once, you've had the guts to ask a straight question, I guess you deserve the truth. I've watched you grow up and become something I detest: a weakling. And don't get the idea that's a snap conclusion I came to when you were thirteen and wouldn't help brand calves. In my mind, I gave you a million breaks. I was always making allowances for what you couldn't or wouldn't do. I beat up on Sam Miller one time about six years ago because he said we should send you to Sweden for an operation to turn you into a girl like you were meant to be in the first place. And don't get the idea I want a pat on the back for that.

"After you were sixteen and you were worse if anything, everything changed for me. To put it pure and simple, I'd had enough of you. I really quit giving a damn what you did. I wasn't going to boot you out or begrudge you money or anything like that. I just quit caring. But you weren't content to let things be. You had to make a big scene at the party.

"Now I may not care about you; but I do care about your mother. And when you start embarrassing her in front of her friends, I get mad. And then I stay mad.

"I know you don't want to go to Europe. You're too big a sissy to ever want to do anything that adventuresome. But I also know that if you don't go, you'll hang around here in spite of hell. And, as long as you're here, you'll be hurting your mother, and I won't let that happen. You must think I'm pretty damned stupid if you thought I'd fall for all that bullshit about you wanting to vote. Your mother would believe anything that made you seem normal, but I don't fall for crap like that. We'd all be starved to death if I was that dumb. Maybe Europe'll make you into a man, though I doubt it.

"Now, are you satisfied?"

I sit for a moment staring at Father. His jaw set ahead with the determination that is his trademark. In work, in business, in protecting my mother. He is casting me out with shot put force. To safeguard what is his.

No use crying that I wish them no harm. No use to say, so I am a coward and all you say. It's still not my fault. That I missed that stage of growing up that is supposed to make a man strong and responsible.

I get up. Father stares moodily at the wall, smoking slowly. Drained of enthusiasm, I start the suddenly long walk to my couch. I stop at the kitchen door and turn to Father. Say, "Thanks." Maybe he knows I am serious, maybe not. But it is probably the sincerest thanks I've given. For the sincerest truth I've heard. Tells me I must leave and find new havens. Gives me a why I cannot argue with. Thank you, Father. For I truly have no right to stay here. Robbing you of all things material and personal. Food and a happy old age. Must be gone. But the inevitable where.

So suddenly my expectations have crumbled. I pushed to get

the last grain of sand through the stricture and, just as I gloated on my success, a stronger force has tipped the hourglass over. To show me what little my tampering has accomplished. There is no refuge. What difference if I go to Europe? Is there any less of a home for me there than here? (A useless problem for those who like to tinker at splitting tiny things yet tinier.) What happiness is left in having my plan succeed? Athena will phone and announce the hatching of the monster's egg which I have so carefully laid. And there will be the temptation to say, so what? So we stay here and I wrestle familiar foes instead of going to Europe to wrestle unknown ones.

Did I ever really expect the world to open its arms? What a stupid occupation it's been for me to diddle with circumstances as if circumstance could alter how I relate to it. I am frozen out of every situation simply because I am hopelessly me.

I suppose I should learn to take these problems out on myself. Instead of humiliating my parents, putting Athena through unnecessary hurdles, and heaping insults on everyone. Just so I could bully my way around the board and return panting to square one. After all my preaching to Athena: We are emotions, not physical aspects of the world around us. So, change as it will, the world can never change us with it.

Another priest is damned for preaching one route to salvation and trying to take another, pleasanter path. Fate must be laughing now that I thought her so easily manipulated. Not that she has so subtly poisoned my future.

15: Making Your Final Decisions

"HELLO, ATHENA."

"You knew it was me."

"Yes."

"You'll never guess what happened."

"No." The irony. The irony.

"Daddy's cut me out of his will."

"Athena, there's a lot I have to tell you."

"Didn't you hear what I said?"

"I've got to tell you something."

"It can wait. This can't. Shut up and listen. Daddy decided he didn't want me to go to Europe with you. You should've heard some of the things he said. But, I don't care. I told him he could keep his dirty old American money. And how you'd told me exactly how lousy the way he makes his living is. Anyway, I've got my ticket and Mother slipped me five hundred on the side so it doesn't matter. As far as him cutting me out of his will, I couldn't care less. I've been more or less independent for years and I'm not going to get less independent as I get older."

"Look, Athena, you don't know that for sure. You've got to know what I'm like before you make all these decisions."

"Don't be silly, Tyrone. What does Uncle Bobby know? Things'll work out. We'll make them."

"Don't say that."

"Look, we can do anything we put out minds to. Don't be so

negative. Anyway, things are going off as scheduled. That's what I wanted to tell you. Are your parents seeing us off?" I give up.

"I don't know. I guess I'd better ask. Mother! Are you coming to the airport?" Mother looks sadly at me, then at Father, and shakes her head apologetically. "No, they're not. Athena, we should have a talk tomorrow before we officially decide to go."

"Tyrone, don't be so damned silly. We decided months ago. Look, do you love me?"

"Yes, but . . ."

"No buts. That's all that matters. We're going. I'll pick you up at nine in the morning. Be ready. I told Daddy I was leaving his stinking little car in front of Moberry's house. You know, Father's golfing partner in Calgary? And he could do what the hell he wanted with it. Now look, I've got a million things to do before the morning, so goodbye. I love you."

"But . . ." Bang!

I TOOK a dream. A false, impossible little dream. And I formed it into a plan. Just as false, but not impossible. I took the plan and impregnated the future with it. Then I fed the incubating thing a series of untested drugs to lessen the pain of myself and all its mothers. I looked through a mental microscope to see how it was progressing and saw, to my horror, myriad hideous children waiting to be born. I, the father; I, the madman claiming to be scientist, made weak efforts to abort these deformed futurelings. But, it had all gone on too long. And now I am condemned to wait for each monster to be born.

"Tyrone, what's wrong?"

"Why do you think anything's wrong, Mother?"

"You may think I'm pretty dumb, but I do know you a little bit. You've been sitting here for the last two hours as if you faced death itself. Don't you want to go to Europe?"

"Not particularly."

"Then why go, sweetheart? You can stay here as long as you want."

"It's all really hard to explain, Mother. I wouldn't know where to begin. But, I have to go."

"I'm sorry everything's worked out so badly for you. I don't know what got into Tom."

"It's not Father's fault."

"I'm sorry we're not seeing you off. I think we ought to." And Mother's voice shoots up and she begins to cry. I put my arm around her, which I've never done before, and say that things will turn out all right. There's no need to cry. Feeling a bit like a cry myself. Mother gets up finally and forces her tightened lips to smile. She goes out to the kitchen. All is again very silent.

Outside it has begun to snow. Reminding us that the world keeps spinning, keeps swimming its lonesome path through space. Nothing on this earth is quite as silent as falling snow. It comes peacefully to close the eyes of the dead world. Hangs on the limbs of evergreens to remind us that they too are mortal. Hangs on me as well, but the lesson is unneeded. I know that I am mortal. More mortal than I credit most men with being.

Big, white flakes that stick on the windows, melt, and run. A white army trooping slowly in, tramping methodically over summer's souvenirs. I, for one, surrender. It will snow at least six inches tonight. And I am beyond hoping it will snow feet, blow, and drift the doors shut. Delaying my departure, regardless of destination, is no pleasure now. There is not even a frantic little hoper. From the Canadian womb I will be born and any time between is just waiting. It might as well be Europe with Athena rather than anywhere alone.

16: You Can Never Be Too Prepared

As a hardened coward, I feel that death is the only certainty. For me, a certainty before I reach thirty. I don't see how anyone can put faith in anything else. There are death traps everywhere. Pollution on the wind to wreck the lungs, to stifle the breathing, to pump the heart beyond the poor organ's limits. (I smoke for protection.) Industrial effluents in our streams. To sneak up on you, subtly poisoning, while you try to relax with a pot of tea. Speeding cars with giant motors and grills like the bared fangs of ravenous animals, streaking down undivided highways with madmen at the controls. Wizened scientists brewing new diseases unconquerable by antibiotics, over Bunsen burners in government laboratories. Raising infested super-rats to parachute into unsuspecting neighbourhoods.

Therefore I have gone to great trouble and worked in great secrecy to complete the following will:

> I, Tyrone Lock, being of sound mind and body do hereby bequeath my worldly possessions as follows:
>
> Item A:
>
> My Truck, having no doubt grown quite accustomed to me and doubtless not wishing at this stage of its life to learn the ways of a new driver, I leave to no one. I wish it to remain parked atop the great hill one mile east of the buildings on my parents' farm, as long as it will under natural forces of wind and water remain thereon. I request

that it never be started save once a year on my birthday. On that date, April thirteenth, it should be started, allowed to warm up, then immediately turned off. Nothing should be done to abate its rusting or otherwise deteriorating, for I feel that it and I shall achieve dust together.

Item B:

My Guitar, I also bequeath to no one. I wish it to be smashed into small pieces and the resulting chips to be scattered.

Items C and D:

My stamp and nail file collections, I bequeath to Miss Athena Till, for reasons she will never understand. Nothing is to be added to either.

Item E:

Any money I may have in my possession at the time of my death may also go to Miss Athena Till. However, if I am forewarned of my death, there will be no such money, as I intend to squander it on perishables.

Item F:

Anything else I might own at the time of my death, I am not the least concerned about. My relatives can fight over it.

signed,
Tyrone Lock

P.S. To my parents I leave nothing for I feel that they may rightfully wish to forget me as soon as possible. I wouldn't want any material objects possessed by me in life to slow that process. I do leave them with these words in the form of an unused epitaph for my grave, which I want to be unmarked and uncared for:

Whatever transpired, I was never attempting to be cruel.

Again, signed,
Tyrone Lock

17: Think of Your Journey as a Rebirth

THIS MORNING finally happened. Right on schedule. Black Monday.

The sun came up in the usual place. Over a horizon which I remembered was the east one. Which of course reminded me that I would be bounding over it in absolutely no time. That I would be sitting in front of one of those white streaks that I see up in the sky. Way, way, way up.

And Athena picked me up. After my last breakfast of Mother-made. Which I had no appetite for. And here I am. Next to an excited Athena. In her little white car. Somewhere between home and Calgary. I haven't been paying much attention to where.

"Are you excited, honey?"

"Trembling with it." I can still see my house fading in the falling snow as we drove away. Descartes might've said it was disappearing off the face of the earth. I might agree. It became first a dark shadow behind an opaque wall, and then the snow choked it invisible.

"Sad to be leaving?"

"Yes."

"You're not very talkative this morning."

"No."

"A little frightened?"

"No." And it's true. I just rattle through the gates like a croquet ball, wherever anyone should choose to knock me.

"I'm as excited as anything! I probably shouldn't be. It's no big thing to be going to Europe. Everyone does it these days. Of all people,

Milly Fredericks told me she's going. Europe will never be the same after suffering her. I'll bet she comes home within two weeks."

I'm drifting along aimlessly, hopelessly. I think Plato was sad. He didn't eat his breakfast very heartily. I mean, he ate it, but he wasn't very spirited about it. Maybe because I threw him about a thousand dog biscuits from my window last night.

"We're going to be in England when they have the Silver Wedding ceremonies. Did you know that? We might see the Queen. I'm really excited. I wonder what they'll feed us on the plane. I heard that you should eat like anything at supper because they serve those skimpy continental breakfasts."

Mother cried a lot. Said she'd miss me. Probably will too in a perverse sort of way. In the self-punishing way that mothers miss sons. Father shook my hand. I guess he had to as part of his fanatical attempt to keep Mother happy. "Tyrone, you're not listening to a single word I'm saying."

"I've got a lot on my mind. Sorry."

"We have to get someone to drive us out to the airport. Or else, we could get someone to drive us out in this car and then leave it back in front of Moberry's."

Athena drives with great zest and ingenuity. Hitting the piles of snow with just enough momentum so that we magically pop out the other side still moving. Steering expertly into each skid like a dog biting its tail. And each time we straighten out, the car gives a little shudder. She should've been a rally driver. Making another mark for the liberation of women. Would look nice even in one of those ridiculous helmets. Her beauty overpowering any apparel.

"Who do you know in Calgary who could take us out to the airport?"

"No one."

"You went to university there for three years. You must know someone."

"I know no one. In the whole world, I don't know a soul."

"Don't tell me you're going to be weird today, Tyrone. We've got too many things to do for you to start that."

"Everything will happen according to an ordered plan. We will be shifted to Europe like digits being subtracted."

"Oh my god, Tyrone, stop it! Honestly, you sound like a mental patient. I hope that's not what I have to expect from you in Europe."

"How do you keep your life so incredibly normal?"

"Well, that's hardly a compliment. I'm sorry if I suddenly strike you as horribly normal."

"There's nothing horrible about being normal."

"Well, even so, I can't answer a question like that."

"No, of course not. No one can. All those books on the subject, too. And not one single, point-by-point, surefire list of instructions on how to be boringly, traditionally normal."

"Tyrone, you're the first person I've ever heard of who got disoriented before the trip began."

So true. The trip into this world has left me disoriented for twenty-two years. Does she expect me to accustom myself to another one in a matter of days or weeks? Unfortunately, I think she does. I am going to go to sleep. I am sick of trying to reason out why this is happening. In some sick mind, it is probably being lauded as Justice. Good old Plato. Not the dog, but the other one. Didn't he put a theory to the fact that our conversations trade in such terms as Justice and Truth without the earthly existence of equivalents? I would have called Plato, the dog, Justice; but it seemed an unfitting name for a dog. The thought behind the christening was that there was no such animal as this puppy I had found abandoned. So I thought, there's no such animal as Justice either. I will call him Justice. But to save him embarrassment with his peer group and a life of constant explanation, I named him after the man who first pronounced on all these things.

It is time to cast my ballot with this ancient philosopher and to go even a step farther. Not only is there no concrete item to point to as the epitome of the Justice we speak of so confidently, but I can never recall a proper example of it either. Is there ever so pure a Justice that it applies to all concerned? Has there ever been a case where what others have called Justice has applied to me? It is just for Father to want me to leave because he values Mother more than he values me. But can I truthfully agree? I cannot put Mother above myself.

To escape all this, Plato decided the Forms must be independent of man. And that may have been the day that fatuous abstraction began. I would label it the Justice-is-but-is-fat-little-good-to-anyone hypothesis. All these ancient thinkers. Their minds are gone, but their thoughts live on in troubled minds such as mine. They left their burdens as I will leave mine, with the difference that no one will bother carting my confusions down the path of generations.

My mediocrity so confirmed, I begin to drop off to sleep.

"TYRONE, WE'RE almost there." Marble statues crawling off their pedestals and marching toward me. Italian Renaissance robots goose-stepping through my head. Glassy, unmoving eyes which, though they are immobile, are somehow fixed upon me.

Shabby, unmerciful dream-life. You had a choice of many pleasant possibilities, things that would have made me happy, but no. Torture him in all dimensions. Harden him to this world that he doesn't matter to. Black his mind's eye.

Away, you beasts! I thrash at them uselessly. They march on, oblivious to anything I do against them.

"Tyrone. Wake up!"

"Wha . . . !"

"You must've been having a bad dream, honey."

"Always are. Bigger foes. Run from anything . . ."

"Snap out of it, Tyrone. You're still half asleep."

Then I am still half tortured. I sit forward and rub my eyes. Still on white roads bonded onto packed tracks. Isn't snowing. Tiny snow wraiths coat the road, making it all seem to move.

"Where in hell are we?"

"Just about there."

"Where?"

"Calgary, silly. It's about another ten miles, but I wanted you to help me decide what we should do with the car and all the rest."

At the moment, I couldn't decide which was my mother and which was the Queen from a selection of photographs.

"Well?"

"Well, what?"

"Well, what should we do with the car?"

"Maybe we could pawn it."

"Jesus, Tyrone, I wish you'd be a little more helpful."

"We'll call a taxi and tell him to pick us up at Whoeverberry's."

"Moberry's. That's not exactly the way to start living on the cheap. Couldn't we ask Sally?" Athena's best friend.

"Taxis don't give me headaches. I will gladly pay for the taxi."

"Well, it's just . . . she and I *are* best friends. I'd like to talk to her before I go."

Time to make a stand, Tyrone. I'll be damned if I will spend my last Canadian hours with Sally, the least likable person I've ever met.

"I'll stand and wait for however long you'd like outside a phone booth while you talk to her. I'll even give you the dime."

"That's not the same and you know it. I'm sorry you two don't get along, but really, I would like someone to see us off. It'll look horrible if we just get on the plane with nobody waving at us."

"To who?"

"To who what?"

"To who will it look terrible?"

"Well, to just everybody, Tyrone. We'd look like nobody cared; or as if we were running off on the sly or something."

"So?"

"So I just want to have a nice, normal farewell where someone's crying and waving. I just want someone to hug and to know that they are sad I'm leaving. Is that all right with you?"

I cannot understand this. Who does care and aren't we running off on the sly? I can't say these things to Athena, gathering that she feels strongly in need of these lies. Sally may cry, but only because her girdle is pinching.

"Sally gives me a great big pain in the ass."

"You give Sally a great big pain in the ass."

"Then we'd probably just as soon not see each other, wouldn't we?"

"Hell, Tyrone! You always spoil everything for me. Is it such a big thing to ask? If I want my best friend there, I shouldn't have to ask you anyway. You're being a big chauvinist pig!" A pause.

"Oink."

"What's that supposed to mean?"

"That I would love to have Sally snivel us on our way."

No one can say that I, Tyrone Lock, am embarrassed to back down in a battle of the sexes.

"Thanks, honey. Will you try and be nice?"

"Can you guarantee that Sally won't say that I make noises when I eat again?"

"Well we won't eat then."

"Eating was just an example. If we don't do anything that I do badly as far as Sally is concerned, we may not be eating, breathing, or moving for several hours."

"Sally's not that bad, Tyrone. She didn't mind your eating after I explained that it's because your teeth don't bite evenly."

"I believe, if I remember correctly, that she asked me, 'What is that awful sound coming out of your mouth?'"

Athena laughs. Big joke. "Lord, you say that funny. You've repeated it at least a thousand times and I still can't help laughing."

"So I repeat myself. Did Sally point that out as well?"

"Oh c'mon, Tyrone, don't dwell on it. And don't, whatever you do, say, 'So I dwell on things, do I?'"

In my mind, I think, so I dwell on things, do I?

But wait; there has to be something better than Sally, on this of all days, with which to fill the thinking space. This day when the lines of my life are zeroing in on each other with such speed and force. Determined to achieve focus before I sleep another night. Where is the videotape of my life story? Which according to tradition should be streaming past my mind's eye? Perhaps that tradition only holds true for those whose life stories are worth remembering.

18: Photography and Souvenirs: Reminiscence Makes Your Voyage Last Forever

WHENEVER I go in search of memories for the purpose of rationalizing my life, I always come up with those segments of my history held down by the ghosts of old girlfriends. That tiny team which altogether would be insufficient in number to represent me in a basketball game.

Those creatures responsible for all my pleasures and most of my problems.

In all cases, I had little to do with their capture. I'm not the type who swaggers suavely into the tavern, knocks his chosen woman over the head with a great psychological club, and drags her off by the metaphysical hair to his metaphorical cave. As opposed to the hunter, I am the bait. I lie in the trap grinning. (Saying "Cheese," if you like.) Waiting and waiting as the trap rusts open.

I will give an example of a typical Tyrone Lock conquest.

She and I arrive in some situation together. Let's say it's in a room at a party which all but us have just vacated. She stays to perhaps powder her nose. I stay most certainly to avoid the company.

I am totally unimpressive, but all the moment has to offer the young lady. So, we talk. I say something miles from being appropriate, like, "Did you happen to ever eat a worm when you were a child?"

She laughs uncomfortably, saying no, and I pursue the subject because for some unsavoury reason I want to know.

"Not even once?"

She says, "No. Why are you asking me all this anyway?" Her

attention being caught, she now wants me to identify myself as a particular class of pervert.

I reply, "I'm doing a survey." She will laugh and think, at least he's a funny weirdo, never realizing that I am fairly serious. Then, she might want my life story in précis and I would tailor it according to what I think she might like. From rare time to time, I am right and she is impressed enough to want to know more. And if there is a lunar eclipse, or Halley's Comet happens to be passing by, our rendezvous might end with her dragging me off to her bedroom. And if both a lunar eclipse and Halley's Comet happen to be happening at once, a romance might begin.

Yes – women conquer me. And so easily too. So at their leisure they have me. I'm so easy.

Athena had me in such incredible fashion, I think I will reminisce about it. Such a pretty memory of how things went in a flash from bad to perfect. I was at a party where I wasn't wanted. Is it hard to imagine that it was in Sally's apartment with its several rooms? A terrible date I had, with a face that for some irretrievable reason reminded me of a peach, had brought me there.

After a long term of hopeless celibacy, I had given myself to believe that this girl who sat next to me in a class, and daily asked questions so stupid that people would turn to look, was incredibly horny. That, in short, after devouring a bottle of travel-sickness pills, I might be able to ease my body's pain on her. So one day, after class, I asked her for coffee and, in complete terror that someone might hear, went on to ask her out. Didn't specify where or to what, assuming I suppose that she wouldn't be choosy.

I arrived to pick her up that night in a nauseated state, but with pockets full of pills to counteract all that. She lived in a two-storey, low-rent slum on Seventeenth Avenue. Which seemed to have fat, acne-ridden girls and skinny cats coming out of every crack and portal. The girls gathered round to investigate their housemate's catch, giggling all the while. She made her Pygmalion staircase entrance in finest, floor-length, creased calico. I reached for my pills.

She asked me where we were going and I confessed that I didn't know (although I was thinking at the time that a dogfight might be appropriate). She said she had a chance to go to a real high-class party, and now that she had a date we might as well.

When we got there and she didn't seem to know anyone, I started to think that her invitation was of the sort where she was sitting at the next table to Sally in the cafeteria when Sally said, "I'm inviting simply everyone." She dragged me around for a while like a security blanket. So, I offered her my thumb to suck and she went away.

Having given in to my usual urge to be cheap, I had brought no liquor. I stood alone, thirsty, and unnoticed for a while, until I started wishing I was drunk more than I was wishing to be thought harmless. I walked up to a table, bowed with the weight of bottles, and picked a whisky I could not afford. I poured two drinks so that those who stared at me might think that someone else was to blame for my being there. Then I found a spot in the hall where the traffic moved continuously enough that I wouldn't be noticed drinking two drinks at once. After a few such journeys into the valley of bottles and unkindly eyes, I was grinning benignly at everyone. A few more, and I was passing them all off as pompous assholes and squirting soda at those who looked particularly severe. One or two more, and I was singing snatches of "Roll Me Over in the Clover" and other boys'-camp classics. Gloating all the while that I was getting plastered on the money of the filthy rich. My own version of Robin Hood. Robbing from the rich and giving to myself. Sticking my straw in the royal vat. But finally, as good things go, I bit my straw flat at the end.

Sally came up to me sociably soused, holding a champagne bottle by the neck, and droned, "The young lady you brought to my party has passed out. She positively reeks of gin. I had Eric, the waiter I hired for this evening, deposit her down the hall in the third room on the left. Who are you with by the way? I don't recall having ever met either of you."

"The invitation was whispered to me by a great peach tree in Heritage Park. I'm sure you know him. He's the fellow who's presently writing his Master's thesis on the role of fruit in the carnivorous economy."

"Would you mind reviving your date and leaving the premises?"

"Charmed."

I rollicked through the smoky fuzz and had the lonely feeling that I was passing through a department store display of manikins. All laughing, ho, ho, with voices deepened by graduate school. I risked strangulation by fallen streamers to gain the hall. And, in the confusion, disremembered which hand I write with and fell headlong into the third room on the right.

The room was lit by only one fat candle on a bedside table. Sitting knees up in a silky gown on the bed, munching cheese and crackers, was Athena. A massive brute wearing a white roll-neck sweater and with thick black hair, professionally mussed, was sitting beside her fondling her foot.

As I made my entry, that historic headlong slide into the home plate, he began to swear with vengeance.

"This night has been a fucking circus! How the hell am I supposed to thaw out an ice block like you with drunken clowns stumbling in here every god damn minute! I'm going to try and find a real party with real women at it!"

He shuffled into his shoes and left, dragging heels over prostrate me. Kick a guy while he's down, I thought. Merciless cad! I raised my head. Through the swimming candle-darkness, I focused on Athena. She wasn't looking at me. She just continued with her cheese and crackers, letting the rest of the world take care of itself.

"God! You're no peach!"

She looked at me where I lay, too paralytic to move anything but my head. A smile appeared. Grew into a grin. Toothpaste-ad teeth. God, I thought, It's the freshest mouth in town! And I entertained the idea that I had died of overexposure to the callousness of the world and was first-glimpsing heaven. Where all the commercials come true. I couldn't believe the world capable of such a girl in such pure candlelight. I thought that by some freak occurrence in the cosmos, I had fallen, Alice-in-Wonderland-style, across the barrier, into celluloid.

"I've never been confused with peaches before. What are you on?"

"There's no confusion at all. Don't tell me how I got here, okay? I never want to be able to leave. Do you mind if I don't move?"

"Help yourself. It's probably very clean on the floor. Sally had a herd of servants vacuuming all day."

"Good that you're letting me not move; because I'm fairly sure that I can't. Who's Sally?"

This made Athena laugh. She flipped onto her stomach and, leaning on her elbows, stared down at me from the bed's edge. I rolled over with difficulty to meet that golden gaze.

"Did you crash this big, high-class party?"

"Not intentionally."

"Have you had fun?"

"Of a sort."

"What sort?"

"Playing Robin Hood."

"How do you play Robin Hood?"

"It's the newest variation on an old theme. I directed and acted. Unfortunately, no one filmed. Robin Hood is characterized as a righter of social injustices done to himself by the wealthy. He would give his bounty to the poor, but he primarily steals liquor and has the noble idea in mind that if he drinks enough, the poor may not get any and be the better for it. He envisions himself as a great funnel depriving the rich and safeguarding the destitute. He is martyring his liver."

Athena had begun to laugh and I thought I could see the sounds that she was making ignite like miniature fireworks in the air. My ears drummed an exotic beat. All tissues titillated, so I continued. "In this particular instance he wheedles himself into the confidence of a girl whose face is much like a peach, hairy and overripe. He asks her out, for she has claimed invitation to a party of the aristocracy. How was R. H. to know that she too was crashing? They arrive at the party and he notes the lack of welcome. Lesser men would have fled, but Robin Hood, and Trusty Siphon and Bloated Liver, his Merry Membranes, forge on. They drink Crown Royal; they drink Scotch; they drink champagne.

"Then they are discovered and told to leave, all because of the lying peach who, being an impostor masquerading as a Merry Membrane herself, has drunk herself unconscious. In her ignorance of the methods of R. H. and his Membranes, she has done so on the waiter's supply of cheap gin.

"The situation comes to look as if all might be lost as Robin Hood skulks to find her and drag her off the premises at the Queen Mother herself's request. But, just as everything is at its blackest, R. H. leaps onto the magic celluloid which bears him to someplace very nice, maybe the halfway house to heaven, where he is presently begging a goddess of no small stature and beauty for a few moments of sanctuary.

"How about it, sweet goddess? Can I pass some time with you? Or should I go back to looking for the peach?"

"You may do as you wish, Robin Hood," she said. "For I was once a princess and very enamoured of thee."

"I did never know that I was blessed with such a royal groupie. I please to stay on this magic rug covering this magic island which floats in peace on this sea of chaos."

Athena lay smiling down and we were silent and staring for a pleasantly passed eternity. Neither of us wanting to burst the dream we had painted around ourselves. Finally, Athena reached down and played her fingers in my forelock and quietly said, "You're the first original drunk I've ever met, Robin Hood."

"You're the first real goddess I've ever met."

"I'm not a goddess. I wish I was."

"I'm not Robin Hood."

"Who are you?"

I told her my name and she said it was a nice name because, I guess, my name is a nice name. People like to mention it when they talk to me because it makes a nice sound; nicer than I am. I asked her who she was and she said her name. It convinced me that she was a goddess after all; a humble one. She asked me to climb onto the bed with her and I somehow did, drawing on a reserve tank with a switch marked "enthusiasm."

"Well, Tyrone, I've spent this evening battling off the quarterback of the varsity squad who is strictly a pig. I'm not frigid but he, in particular, makes me sick. I didn't think he would. That's why he was in here in the first place. He left when you came in saying I was an ice block because his ego was starting to collapse."

"Under a barrage of cheese and crackers."

"Exactly. Want some?"

We munched until the plate was crumbs only. "All gone," she said and lay back as I had done. We stared at the ceiling; she, I suppose, because she wanted to, and me only because I wasn't sure she would appreciate me perusing her inch by inch.

"Tyrone, we have been here for about twenty minutes and you haven't made a pass at me. Why not?" I shrugged. "Most football players would've had me semi-raped ten times by now."

"I'm not an athlete as you may have guessed by my graceful entrance."

"Well, you are a man. A kind of cute one at that. What's really neat about you is that you look good lying down. Most guys, when the lie down, look like their heads are swollen or something. Really super-handsome guys, a lot of them, too. It's repulsive. But you, you just look sweet and sort of sleepy. C'mon, tell me why you haven't attacked me."

"Well, because I am a serf and you are a goddess, or at very least, royalty. And, if I were to attack you, you might not let me stay and I might never see you again. You might even hate me for touching you and I would then hate myself and life would be purposeless." I wonder if Athena ever realized that that statement was scarcely exaggeration. She laughed, I remember.

"What's a sweet guy like you doing here?"

"At the moment, thanking all sorts of things for the privilege."

She rolled over and put her head beneath my chin. Wrapped her body round me and lay silent. All the cells in my body were trying to emigrate to the privileged side. And for a long while we did not move. Then she rose to kiss me and a series of slow crescendos began. Each one breaking in a wider splash than the last. We graduated with sloth-like slowness to a wonderland of duets. The combination of mind and body in both of us. The combinations of our minds; our bodies. Two cubed makes eight slices off heaven's loaf. Somewhere along this splendid line, there was a pause, breath-length, when Athena locked the door and confirmed the night.

"WHAT ARE you thinking, Tyrone? Usually when we're in the middle of the city, you're in a state of panic. You've been staring out the window with a silly grin on your face for about the last twenty minutes."

"I was thinking about the night I met you."

"Thinking about Sally, huh?"

"No, just you."

"Why bother thinking about me six months ago when you can talk to me right now?"

"It was such a beautiful night."

"Don't you love me as much anymore?"

Hesitation at a time like this could result in tears and battery in mid-traffic.

"Of course I do," I lie, "I wouldn't think of that night as such a nice memory if I didn't."

Athena is pacified. I look at her, still goddess-like, but so bound to earth. A saint minus her halo, and that is the difference between now and more glorious then.

Foolish women that must be constantly reassured that your passion for them hasn't fallen off a degree. They must know that if all men kept up their first flush of passion, civilization would have died of neglect long ago. I suppose it gives them a feeling of strength to be always able to bully us into that particular lie. What I feel for Athena has gone through all the pitiful changes that aging loves are subject to. Our love is like a wall of affections and dependencies which we paint and repaint many times in many colours. And the combination of colours is never as bright or distinctive as the original hue. But the layers upon layers give that same wall a frightening strength. I could have left Athena after that first night and suffered her loss for only months. But now, her loss would murder my future. Leave it as empty and cold as an ancient tomb.

"Are you sure it's all right that Sally comes with us?"

"Why not? In a way, I owe her a great debt. If she wasn't as insufferable as she is, I might never have met you."

"Oh, Tyrone, we would have met. Don't you believe in Fate?"

More than I dare say. The meddlesome monster! I have experienced joyful days only when she was busy deceiving and disrupting others. Fate delights in creating anarchies only she can thread reason through.

"I would sooner trust in Sally."

"Oh yes, I'd forgotten about Tyrone Lock's eccentric conception of Fate. You've told me often enough, I'm surprised I was able to forget. Maybe with a huge effort of will, I'll be able to forget again."

"We'll get Sally if you want her."

I SHALL never forget the look on Sally's face when Athena and I walked out of the room next morning. Or rather, afternoon. I could have been a herd of maggots coming at her the way she jumped. I thought she was going to leap to the phone and call the police on this bumpkin who had somehow tampered, no doubt illegally, with the virtue of her friend. And then, Athena introduced us. She said, "Sally, I'd like you to meet the sweetest guy ever to come into my life. Tyrone Lock."

Sally held her distance of about ten feet so as not to catch whatever I had that had made me so poor.

"I think we've met. I seem to remember asking you to relieve the premises of that unconscious woman you brought here."

"Is she still here?" I asked.

"No. About six of us almost developed hernias transporting her to a taxi."

Athena asked, "The Merry Membrane?" And I nodded sadly. Thinking that I would then be chucked into a similar gutter.

"You little heartbreaker, you. Well it's just too bad for her, because I'm not letting you go. Finders keepers."

So funny to think back to that old confusion. That Athena thought she was finding the lost penny when actually she was only in possession of the loser. Meanwhile, Sally was looking about for Athena's lost mind. Hoping she would find it soon, so that she could be rid of me and have the apartment aired and checked for crawling things. The only question that she asked, in hopes that there might be a possible excuse for the absence of Athena's common sense, was the traditional one:

"Are you an artist?"

"Of a sort," I replied, not feeling confident enough to indulge myself with truth telling. But Sally's a born niggler. Never satisfied with the surface generalization, she digs until she finds the dirt.

"What type of artist are you?"

"Well, I take old telegrams and cut out the letters. I paste them on various parts of my naked body, then pose in front of a mirror and compose music out of the first thing that crosses my mind. I'm afraid I haven't any of my work with me at the moment."

Athena laughed a lot, I recall. But Sally was grim. My future in that many-roomed penthouse so high above the ground seemed slim. Still under the impression that Athena lived there, I was cherishing the minutes until I was shunted down the elevator shaft. To lie broken with the other toys who I imagined would be wearing smiles on their cracked heads.

But, soon after, Athena packed up and drove me to her apartment, a little more modest, where she lived alone. Sally kept a room in her penthouse for whenever Athena wished to stay. The amazing convenience of affluence. In Athena's flat, I lived in luxury for the remainder of the university year. She bought me clothes and shaving equipment, all so I would never have to return to my own jungle of a room for fear I would be tempted to stay. Small chance of me being quite that demented. For a while, Athena splurged, and a pretty little German maid brought us breakfast in bed and packed us university lunches. Athena read my books to me while I lay in her lap in the evenings and I absorbed those thin, unglamorous facts as if they were the sweetest nectar. Athena could make Microeconomic Theory sing in my ears. I became an A student, invited to graduate school by my professors, who all thought me dedicated. Saw me as suffering nightly in the library, a pile of books around me, so high it obscured me from all distraction. It makes me wonder if Karl Marx and Lord Keynes had Athenas stashed away to inspire them to revolutionary thought.

So sad, when summer came and her father invited her to learn the Protestant work ethic the hard way in her home town by packaging chickens at the local plant. He said it would give her a greater respect for his money, which she spent like water. I suspect there was more devious thinking involved. I suspect that, communicated from the long tongue of Sally, were degrading stories about me and my apparently unblemished mediocrity, and the way I had forced myself into Athena's life. Sally has always felt the weight of guilt upon herself for bringing Athena and me together. No matter how indirect her role actually was, she feels chiefly responsible and endeavours with every fibre to put asunder what no man should have joined.

But all that failed. The more they tried to get rid of me, the closer Athena stuck to me. For reasons all, including myself, were at a loss to understand.

And now, as a culmination of all that gilt-edged recent history, we are parking in front of Sally's apartment building once again. Perhaps to close this little book. Pray now that it is Volume One and that there will be continuing adventures of Athena and Tyrone to come.

Athena smiles at me and I must look a pitiful sight preparing myself for Sally. Where my ego will be mercilessly tortured and sacrificed. Then offered to the lowest bidder. "Hello Salvation Army? Have you time to pick up a nose-picking package of bumpkin? He has been meddling in high society as if he could ever fit into it. We would like him to be re-conscripted into the army of the poor."

19: An Equipment Supplement: Steel-Toed Hiking Boots

CURBED IN the shadow of Ballymount Towers. Athena opens her door and presses the button that pops her seat belt back into its socket.

"Are you coming up?"

"No."

"All right then. We won't be long." Athena disengages her long self. Stands for a second beside the car. Hesitating. Reintroduces her face to my view and says, "Try to be nice to Sally, Tyrone. Please? She's had a hard life these past few years and you should try to humour her."

"A hard life? Why, did the butler quit? Or has she been breaking a lot of fingernails lately?"

"Don't be nasty. You know exactly what I mean. Her last two affairs have gone very badly and she needs all the sympathy she can get."

"Only because she attracts her own type."

"Tyrone! Please!"

"I will be so nice you may be sick."

"You may wind up sick if you're not."

The door slams on that threatening note and Athena trots with Amazonian agility into the mouth of Ballymount Towers.

I am not expecting a quick return. Athena and Sally haven't seen each other for possibly two weeks and will have hours of secrets to swap. Of the deepest, darkest variety. I'm glad to be confided in so little.

Sally may, at this moment, be dampening Athena's shoulder with her latest story of misuse and rejection. Telling how the quarterback of the varsity team ran a few touchdowns on her and then hiked her to the second-string place-kicker.

A hard life these past few years! Hah! I suppose she had a twinge of anxiety that terrorized her. "Egad! I felt something! Someone has been committing alchemy on my heart! Changing it back into flesh!"

Buck up, Sally. It's a long way to the bottom of the varsity ladder. It may take you several baccalaureates to get down to the water boy or the balding coach. Perhaps it will take an entire Master's before you find yourself stowing away in a locker full of discarded jockstraps. A lowly training-camp follower.

I must stop this if I am to obey my orders.

But what if Sally had my problems? How would she deal with my brand of terror? At this stage of my dilemma, she would be on a cardiac machine. Whereas I, I will probably save my stroke for takeoff.

Takeoff! Only a matter of hours now until I am buffeted by strange smells, eating strange foods, being shoved and elbowed by masses of strange-looking people who insult me in strange accents. Until I am seeking solace in foul-tasting, unmentholated cigarettes and warm beer. Not knowing where I am or where to go. Looking to the left for the car that comes upon me from the right.

And it's known as a Holiday! A European Excursion. The unsurpassable in edible education. The key to erudition. Come with us to Europe and mingle with wonderful, exotic disease germs. Enjoy the fabulous view of Tower Bridge from the window of your ward in the London Free Hospital. Actually feel the austerity of this vision as victims of the Black Plague may once have done. Spend eternity lying beneath a mossy stone in a beautiful English country churchyard. Choose your epitaph now while stocks last.

> Doomed, doomed,
> Fucked and doomed,
> Before me dark
> The future loomed.

I hated this city while I was living here and now I look out on even it as if it were some vast playground where I once swung and slid.

There, the university. Where three years were squandered. Achieving a BA that I would be far too embarrassed ever to place behind my name.

There, behind that hill, the Safeway. Where many a Revel was squeezed.

There, the Foothills Hospital. Where I was fired from my position as a summer replacement janitor. By a shrieking little woman, angry to the point of tears. Who said I was the laziest, most incompetent person she had ever met. All because my floor polisher got out of hand one day and went screaming into the side of the hot dinner wagon causing it to eject forty-five prescription lunches. All made slightly worse by the fact that as the polisher made its unmanned flight, it pulled the cord tight behind itself and tripped a little old lady who happened to be standing near by. And who had to be carried off on a stretcher due to a severely disabled hip. All of which was blamed, without mercy, on me.

There, McMahon Stadium. Where I once passed out from too much rum during the third quarter of a Calgary–Edmonton game. And was tossed, with a minute remaining in the match, onto the field at about the one-yard line by those whom I once called friends.

And now that I am finally able to look at my Calgarian history almost amusedly, I must depart. In the belly of a great airplane. Never to return in anything but a box.

Suddenly, the door is opened and Athena is in. Grinning widely. Sated with salty secrets. Sally leans through the open door behind her.

"Hello, Tyrone. It's good to see you."

In a pig's ear.

"Good to see you too, Sally. How's the football team doing this year? Ouch!" Athena has just ground her heel on my toes. Thought that her putting her foot there when she got in was a matter of romantic touching.

"Sally said she'd be glad to drive us to the airport. Isn't that nice of her, Tyrone?"

"Eager to get rid of us, eh Sally? Ha. Ha. OUCH!" Is that the oozing warmth of blood in my shoe? "What's wrong? Oh, I just have a little cramp in my lung. Must be cancer. I should get that part cut off, I guess. Ouch!"

"My favourite aunt died of lung cancer, you know."

"Oh, did she? That's a shame." Athena is glaring at me.

"Well, I guess we should get going, Tyrone. If you know what I mean?"

Athena starts field-marshalling us everywhere. Sally there. Tyrone here. Rover lie down. Rover fetch stick. Tyrone roll over and prepare for a kick. You go in your car, we'll go in mine.

"Why, Tyrone? You said you were going to be nice."

"I think my toes are bleeding."

"Good!"

"I was trying to be nice."

"My ass! You couldn't say one thing without insulting her. That's exactly how hard you were trying! I ask very little of you, Tyrone, and you always manage to give me less."

Athena is driving fit to kill. Cutting in and out of traffic, slamming through her gears, to gain a couple of car lengths per stoplight. I look back and Sally has disappeared in the confusion. I confess that I am hoping she has had an accident.

"Sally has disappeared."

"She knows the way," Athena snaps. I wish that abruptness of voice was not there.

Sooner than is safe, we are at Whoeverberry's, pulling in down the street from their overgrown house. Athena bashes her fingers on the dashboard. She will not speak to me. Don't hate me too much, Athena. Take heart in the fact that you will never lose me to your best friend. You will be spared that particular Harlequin plot. I am as confident as it is possible for me to be that Athena could never put Sally ahead of me. But, there is more at stake here. If my meagre knowledge of women serves me correctly, she may even be a little pleased that I am so unimpressed with Sally. She is upset, however, because I have disobeyed a direct order. She thinks back to when I would have trotted off that balcony for her, and says to herself, Tyrone doesn't love me as much. Just proves that love wounds the mind as opposed to murdering it.

But, time shouldn't be lost in healing this rift. Cover up the initials in the cement before it hardens and wears the scar forever. Must gather up my tact. Show eloquence. Weigh each word against its possible consequence. At a moment like this, the judge and prosecution are one. Facts and blatant evidence are purposeless. Emotions will decide. Heartstrings must be played tunes upon.

"I'm sorry, Athena, for being offensive to your friend. But only because she's your friend. I didn't say those things to her with any thought of injuring your feelings. You see, I always expect good things around you. I expect that all your friends will be nice, that your family will be magnificent. Friends of it too, just because they've known you. So, it's hard for me to imagine someone like Sally as your friend. And sometimes, I accidentally forget. Do you see what I mean?"

"Haven't a clue. But it sounds awfully sweet. Give me a kiss."

I do and the injury is bandaged. And up roars Sally. Stops up the block about a hundred yards. Her back-up lights come on and Sally's sports car squeals at us doing possibly a hundred. I cover my eyes and a little squeak of fear escapes my lips. More screeching of tires. I am too young to be maimed in a parked car.

"Jesus!" shouts Athena and there is a crash. We bounce up in the air a bit and flop down. I have almost had a heart attack. I slowly uncover my eyes. Sally is out of her car, staring at the wreckage. We get out of the car. Sally's sports car is perched atop Athena's bumper. The headlights are gone. Bits of glass on the ground testify to their former presence.

"That's the second time I've done that this month. Daddy's simply going to have to get me a car with better brakes. Sorry about your car, Athena."

"It doesn't matter, Sally. It's only going back to Daddy."

Do all rich women call their fathers Daddy? Defined as an enormous wallet feeding into a cheque book with countless pages. I look up the street and a waddling Mr. Moberry is coming down to investigate the commotion.

"What a nice surprise! Athena and Sally! My, my." He looks at me. "I don't believe we've met."

"We have. You must have forgotten."

"May forget the odd name, but never forget a face. A little talent you need in my business. No, I'm sure we haven't met." Have it your own way, you forgetful old fool. "This is Tyrone Lock, Mr. Moberry. He's my 'fella,' as you of the older generation call them."

"Ha. Ha. We of the older generation. Ha. Ha. Glad to know you, Tyrone." Shake a paw and smile, yes. It certainly is a pleasure to shake your pudgy palm again, sir.

"Looks like you girls have had a bit of an accident. Any idea who owns the other auto?"

"That's mine, Mr. Moberry. I was waiting for Sally. When she got here, this happened."

"No problem, then, is there? Otherwise you might've had to go through all that messy insurance adjusting. I was in a way expecting you, Athena. I had a call this morning from your father."

"Mr. Moberry, it's no use trying to talk me out of going to Europe. I've decided and that's that."

"No, nothing of the sort! He just told me that you'd be leaving your car outside and would I watch it."

"That's all he said?"

"Just a few other incidental things. We may go to California at Christmas to shoot some golf. We hashed that out a bit."

"Golf?" Athena sounds bewildered.

"Is anything wrong, honey?"

"No. Nothing. We must be going now. Thanks for looking after the car. Tell Daddy I'm sorry it got all smashed."

"Well, you have a nice time in Europe. Good that you're going while you're young. We can never seem to get away for more than a few weeks."

Desperate situation, I think. Hardly enough time to get a suntan on the Riviera. Poor fellow. Athena gives him a peck on the cheek. He shakes my hand again. Perhaps a fixation about fingers.

A great consultation begins on how to affix the packs on Sally's ski rack. Sally would no doubt prefer that the luggage went in the back seat and I was tied to the roof. Mr. Moberry and I lift Sally's car off Athena's bumper and Mr. Moberry goes limping off homeward complaining loudly of pains in the back and abdomen. I am smiling, wishing him a happy hernia.

I am stuffed into the back seat. The pilgrimage begins again. All of a sudden, Athena is crying all over the place. Sally asks what's wrong before I can, so as to make me look callous.

"Daddy doesn't care, Sally! He didn't even try to get Mr. Moberry to talk me out of going! He doesn't care!"

"He does too, Athena. He's just using an old psychological trick on you. Daddy tried it once too. When I was arrested for possession of drugs. When I phoned from that awful police station he told me it was my problem and I could see about solving it myself. But, he bailed me out after two hours. Don't worry."

Athena weeps on. I hope death solves these mysteries for me. The first thing I will ask, if there is anything to ask, is a detailed summary of what reasoning lay behind thinking of this sort. Athena now cries where formerly she suggested she could laugh. I am too tired to try and see sense in that. "Why don't you comfort Athena, Tyrone? She's been crying halfway across the city and you haven't said a word."

"A word."

"I don't think that's very amusing."

"Sally, shut up. Athena, I would say something to you about your crying except for the fact that I can't see why you are."

"Tyrone, Daddy doesn't care about me. He cares more about his silly old car."

"Sally's right. It's just a trick to make you not go. But, if you'd sooner not . . ."

"I'm going! That's that! Even if Daddy doesn't care."

How absurd that, all in this week, my father has told me he doesn't care after long pretending that he did, and now, Athena's father pretends not to care for her when he actually does. Did it never occur to anyone that life might be simpler if everyone told the truth? Fine one I am to judge on this issue, having seldom experienced truth-telling. But, if it were the convention to be truthful, I would have never had cause to lie. A world of lies has made it necessary for me to lie as well.

The airport is now in sight. The glamour of the advertisements buried under snow. It looks forlorn and shabby. Rows of taxis cough visible exhaust. We get out of the car and as we untie the packs from the rack, Sally stands back ten feet snapping Polaroid photos. She rips them out, watches them develop, and Athena and I look at our dismal selves. Me at rehearsal for my funeral. Athena, red-eyed with grief over the loss of the great gilt-edged umbilical cord. A fine pair. Sally thinks they are wonderful and keeps snapping. Undoubtedly, so that she doesn't have to help in any way.

"Those showed the serious determination of the adventurer, don't you think? Let's have some now of the two of you smiling. You know, eager for the expedition to begin."

I stand suffering Sally's gaze through the little window and showing my teeth through the forced oval of my lips. Acres of film later, we arrive inside the airport.

We weigh our luggage and it disappears down a conveyor belt. Tickets are stamped and stapled and things are attached. We go off to the bar with an hour to go.

The talk is very small. I drink whiskies because I have arrived at the realization that soon I will be thirty-five thousand feet in the air. My stomach seems to be rippling like a cow's skin when she is ridding herself of flies. All talk is whys and wheres and hows, and although Athena has said nothing to me, she seems to have planned the whole trip in detail. It was merciful of her not to ask me to help. Athena sees me trying to get soused and we are off to the restaurant. Where I request a loaded hamburger and French fries. Was tempted to ask for an extra helping of grease. When it comes, I pour ketchup all over everything and gobble. Sally winces as my jaw pops rhythmically, but she says nothing. Mouth full, but closed, I smile at everyone. Sally and Athena are digging deep in the conversation bucket for crumbs.

I look at my watch. Fifteen minutes. Athena is reminded and we leave for the gate. Security precautions prevent Sally from following us any farther. Good old skyjackers!

"Now, be sure and write, Athena, and tell me everything that happens. I'm thinking of going myself after I finish my degree and I want to know what the other side of Europe is like. All I ever saw on vacation with my parents were cathedrals and fancy hotels. I'm so excited for you."

And now the time has arrived. Sally and Athena are weeping all over each other. We move off. Waving bye-bye.

20: All Set? Then Bon Voyage

As Sally vanishes behind the wall, we are arranged into rows. Showing our tickets to men in blue. Frisked by a little man in green. Who slides a beeping machine up and down my sides. Checking for guns and knives and bombs and other items judged unnecessary for flight-time amusement.

Now we are sitting in a little pen. The huge jet outside whines and howls. I see its bulk through arrow-slit windows. I feel as if I will faint if asked to stand.

"This is so exciting! You'd think with all that money Daddy has I would have flown before. Imagine being our ages and never having been on an airplane. Gosh, it's exciting!"

I look at this pen full of ordinary people. Puffing madly on cigarettes and cigars. Sitting very straight. So pensive, they give the impression that they are holding their breath. So this is excitement.

The intercom shouts us aboard and we launch into line-up. My knees wag like dogs' tails. Into a stuffy little tunnel. Claustrophobia intense and everywhere. Then we are aboard and being ushered along between the seats. We sit. Mine is by the window, Athena beside me.

"Lucky you! Got the window seat."

All the better to die of fear as the ground disappears from reasonable sight. In a fit of chivalry, I offer to trade. Athena says no. I got the window seat fair and square. I insist and we switch. Under the agreement that we will switch back. And there we sit for maybe hours. As systems are checked over and over for flaws, as if they would know when they found one. To putter the time away, I read the emergency precautions guide and look inside the air-sickness bag to see if traces of previous passengers remain. Life jackets and parachutes and emergency exits are cleverly hidden to give us, the passengers, a false sense of living-room security. I am not fooled.

The stewardesses flit about, smiling assuringly at everyone. Now they are getting out the safety equipment and modelling it as an intercom describes its use and location.

Athena watches transfixed. She thinks of all the movies she has seen. Where the stars boarded just such a jet as this. As the first step in another epic search for romance and adventure. And now, she is stepping into that limelight. On the threshold of the great cinematic dream.

I confess there are movies on my mind as well. I see skyjacking; crash landings; equipment failures; pilots disabled by food poisoning. People leaping into life rafts; the odd one missing and going down into the briny deep. The unfortunate victim of the margin for error.

I ignore completely, as this recorded voice confidently drones on, the inevitably happy endings of the movies. They are made to solace the audiences and I refuse to be so buttered up. I am too conscious of all those who have perished in air disasters. And even if it is a minority who meets with any misadventure on airplanes, my ability to tease out Fate's most miscreant nature makes this particular trip a hazard to all upon it.

Have I no public duty to advise them to postpone their trip? To reshuffle their personal dice which have rolled them my unfortunate score?

We are now moving backwards. Pushed by a motored beast with giant wheels. It pulls away from us and our great engines fire. We roll unassisted now, down the cement track.

We sweep in a slow arch and bits of my life are broken off by the edge of this window. The Calgary Tower, the downtown skyscrapers, the cliffs above the Bow River; the night lights at McMahon Stadium, the university's several towers. All gradually vanish into memory. My mind wipes away all blemishes from my Canadian past. Leaving something like an elongated Christmas. Now ending.

I'm swept away by a tidal wave of nostalgia. Pressing sadness-tinged impulses in a great roar up my spine. Flushing my face hot as if I sat before an open fire. But there are no goodbyes. No words. No tears. All the feeling locks itself behind these walls. And for this moment, I am a goodbye. Every cell devoted to the word in all its meanings. Like a man so filled with music that a keyboard lacks purpose. I do not hint at the extent of my farewell.

We speed up. Faster and faster, until my connection with my homeland is only a blur. This machine shrieks as it pours its strength into lift-off. Buckled in, we are pressed to our seats. The nose lifts and for a few more seconds the wheels bump. Then nothing but the steady pull. I glance out. The Calgary Tower points up at us like the finger of the city mentioning our departure to its parts. The hills stretch far away, but there is no chance in the haze of my hoped-for farewell glimpse of the Rocky Mountains.

Then, the plane turns its flaming ass to Calgary and shoots upwards into thinner air. Athena is smiling, so satisfied. As if she has achieved a great thing in losing touch with Canadian soil. I feel a hint of fury and then subside.

Suddenly we strike twisting air currents and the plane shudders like an old auto on cobblestones. I want to scream. If someone else would take the initiative, I would gladly harmonize. The wing tips flutter like bits of cardboard. So this is the end.

I look at the others. All, including my Athena, are shamming confidence that it is only momentary. Glancing at each other knowingly. Saying, turbulence. All nod as they bounce like seeds in a child's rattle. Their placid expressions say, they wouldn't have stuck us up here if there was any danger. Tell that to the doctor who hacked out my appendix. If I scream, they will all decree me a Chicken Little. Let them, I think, as I shriek to myself, The Sky Is Falling! The Sky Is Falling!

A voice over the intercom joins the pandemonium, "This is your pilot speaking. We are encountering a bit of turbulence. There is no need for worry. We will gain altitude as soon as possible and be above it shortly. Thank you."

More knowing nods.

All is suddenly smooth. I sheepishly glance at Athena, and again that look of ill-gotten satisfaction is on her face. She says, "Wasn't that fun?"

Whee! I think. I haven't had such fun since I saw the film about Auschwitz.

And from then on it is smooth. To the extent that it is difficult to decipher any movement at all. We are fed and badgered eternally by a liquor wagon. I make no attempt to refuse.

Every time I chance to look out and see the unnatural platter-like terrain with its blue veins and white patches, my gorge knots tight and I suffocate a second. For Athena, there is the discomfort of hordes of balanced excitements. She is afraid to look one place for fear of missing a jackpot experience in another.

As we speed away from the sun, we smack rather suddenly into deep darkness and I am glad of the blackened windows. But now, my stomach begins to bite me. At first, I think that I may have raced a giant ulcer to completion. But soon the ache becomes familiar and I know that I have poured bad combinations of food and drink into myself and that they are exploding into gas. The ache grows bigger and bigger and the series of greasy foods and liquors and confections that have passed into me are shone like slides on my mind's eye. All looking hideous.

Filled with dietary regrets, I move around and fiddle with the angle of my seat in search of a phantom comfort.

"Tyrone, you're fidgeting!"

"I'm uncomfortable."

"Well, I gathered that. Relax, for heaven's sake. Go to sleep or something."

A fresh bit of humour. That I could sleep with this bomb slowly exploding in my belly. I excuse myself down the aisles of people. A few are rollicking drunk. Others sleep beneath their coats. I wait in line, holding my breath on the discomfort. This straightness of posture has compressed the great bubble and the pain is even more intense. What relief it would be to rid myself of this mass of blocked-up air. Wink at the fellow behind me, pointing at the woman in front. But I cannot. I imagine my digestive systems and they turn up in my mind as fleshy reproductions of old high-school diagrams. I see them glued and clogged by disgusting substances too fast in coming down to be properly processed.

Finally, my turn arrives and I am in the little cubicle. The air vents scream and I point them to blow into my hair as I sit down on the seat. No wonder there are lineups for these tiny havens! How I would love to rest here for the remainder of the flight. Athena would have me searched for, however, or the next ones in line would hammer on the door and shout, "Have a little respect for the bladders of others."

The pain is still there, but an easier burden in this airy confine. I can breathe out and revel in the split-second relief. My lower intestines are giving little quarter. And, as I sit here bound at the ankles by my rumple of clothes, I see the fresh paradox that Fate has worked on this victim. Seeing that I expected her to murder me in myriad horrifying ways on this flight, she twisted a few screws and gave me a bumper case of gas instead. She must be laughing mightily to herself as she watches me now. "Look at the fool! Expected the drama of fire and twisting metal and screaming people. And there he sits, enthroned and fartless."

At last, there does come a knock on the door, a plaintive inquiry, and I must go. I am back beside Athena who queries my lengthy stay. What can one say? It turned out to be a double-flusher? The pain remains little eased. I try to read. Lighting one cigarette from another.

"You'll have lung cancer before we get there at the rate you're smoking, Tyrone."

I list boredom, immobility, tiredness, and insurmountable addiction as excuses for why I am giving my lungs a quick rot. Of course, I don't mention that it gives illusory relief to my near-ruptured abdomen. How unfortunate that gas pains are not something that you can complain of. I remain silent, and even that adds a dimension to my discomfort. I must sleep. Although I don't think it possible. I suggest to Athena that she join me, but she is too absorbed in her fantasies of some life greater than anything we've known. I close my eyes and wait impatiently for my senses to be stunned by drowsiness. I hear Athena's voice talking to another. I peek out beneath one lid and see that it is a polished and dapper man of forty on her other side. All part of Athena's search for the new adventure. This will not assist my release from wakefulness. I suppose I have become a sordid sight. Fighting around on top of this mountain of gas, dressed in my clothes for all seasons. I am not out of any popular suspense novel. Nor the stuff of movies. So, Athena turns to this older gentleman hoping for a tale of intrigue. That perhaps he is a spy. Maybe she would settle for his being a filmmaker.

I dread this trip so much. I know this moment is symptomatic of things to come. As the first damaged cell is to a cancer. How long until Athena tosses this burden overboard and streaks off into dreams? I am in a misery of pain. The physical melting into the mental until I cannot discern between the two. They come to focus deep inside me where some core of rottenness is trying to destroy me.

A wailing choir sings me to fitful sleep.

A TIME that seems a year's length later, I am revived. That time shrinks black-magically to a second when I hear the roar of the plane and see the rows of seats, like symmetrical cells. All unchanged. I look at Athena and her eyes are still wide open. She sees me roused and says nothing.

"How long did I sleep?"

"An hour and a half. We're only a half hour out of London."

There is a tone of great bitterness. My god, has the old viper taught her to hate me already?

"What's wrong?"

"Nothing. There's nothing wrong."

If she had said, "Don't be so stupid," or something like that, I might believe her. But these words are ice-cold. I must know what is wrong.

"No, c'mon. What's wrong? I can tell from your voice that something is. Tell me."

"You farted!" she whispers sharply.

I admit to myself that the gas is gone. So that's where. Into this can of people. Quickly ventilated, no doubt. I laugh.

"Is that all?"

"Is that all! How could you be so vulgar! I've never been so embarrassed in my entire life!"

"Well, I couldn't help it, could I? Are you absolutely certain you've never farted in your sleep?"

"Ssh! Someone will hear. I'm humiliated!"

I burst into laughter as uncontrollable as my twilight indiscretion.

"Was it a loud one?"

"Tyrone! How can you laugh?"

"How can you keep from laughing?"

"I don't think it's a bit funny! I was right in the middle of this conversation with a very nice man too. It was terrible!"

This doubles me up. I imagine Athena listening attentively to this well-tailored guru, as he reminisces about safaris in deepest Africa. And then, my sphincter shouts. Athena blushes. Aging businessman grins as if to say, "Is he with you?" And Athena must bear the shame of me. Now there is a bit of justice.

"Good heavens, Tyrone, would you stop? I didn't think your sense of humour was this bad."

"If only Sally had been here . . ." And I'm off in another fit of aching laughter. "'What's that beastly sound coming out of your . . .'"

"Tyrone, quit it!"

My laughter winds down like a morning alarm and I am too exhausted to finish.

"What happened to breakfast?" I ask.

"I didn't wake you for it. In fact, it was right in the middle of breakfast that you chose to be such a pig."

I find this terribly funny too, but my laughing jag is finished. Squelched by exhaustion and the fact that in her silly, overdignified way, Athena will hold this against me.

"I will call a meeting of my alimentary tract and my subconscious and scold them severely."

Athena does not answer. And I am eaten by sickness at her silence. She is in no mood for me at the moment.

It's no use. Whatever hold I do have on her, power is not in it. I haven't the strength to force her words now or her love ever. And for this I must suffer. She gives and takes like a deity and my part in our love is small. Almost insignificant. If she chooses to unburden herself of me, my shouts of contradiction will echo unanswered. When I am gone from her heart, she will neither see me nor hear me.

"Now you're crying. What is with you today, Tyrone?"

"I'm not crying. It must be the altitude. There's a connection between the ear and the eye. Aggravation of one causes aggravation of the other."

In my mind, the parallels drawn are different. I tell myself that tears and laughter are close sisters. Spring from a common mother-feeling. Tears are merely a few drops of profound depression getting over the dyke.

A general excitement is working its way through the plane. People announcing to other people that we are about to land. The other people replying that they already know. And then we are told to fasten our seat belts. Everyone does so, expertly, trying to make up for the anxious minutes they spent in Calgary attempting desperately to master the mechanism. I am again in terror. Less terrifying, however, for the fact that it is growing familiar. Am getting quite used to the feeling that I will soon be dead. Like a wartime bomber pilot in the deadly routine of boarding for his manyeth mission.

We begin a slow descent. Now into heavy cloud. It is a rising fog, black with the city's waste. I greet this as an omen. Then we break through its floor above a panorama of lights. There is a great oohing and aahing. Athena stares out upon it with mystic quietness, As if Heathrow Airport were the gates of heaven and she dare not speak for fear of seeming less than awestruck. We fall towards the rows of orange lamps. I die a little with each foot of decreasing altitude.

We strike the cement with a force exaggerated by my nerves. There is a terrific roar of brakes and my mind rivals it with shrieks. Responding to a sudden and peculiar urge, I turn to Athena and say, "Let's see if we can get a bag of airsickness to send to Sally as a souvenir of the flight." And as I look at Athena's painfully wrinkled brow, there is a bump and we are in London.

21: The Initial Letdown: Discern Between Disappointment and Disorientation

I LIE here in this freezing, damp hotel bed for which I am paying an exorbitant sum. I don't really know how much it is, but I am sure it is exorbitant. It is gloomy in this subterranean niche and that so-foreign smell that permeates this city seems to have concentrated here. Athena lies beside me very soundly asleep, played out completely by all the concentration she put into coming here. I am awake though my mind is dull and spinning with exhaustion. I loathe the time when Athena will wake and say, "Let's be off to explore." I would sooner hide in this clammy hole than be out there.

Everyone runs in this city! Looking at no one. Impersonal as machines. Was almost trampled to death peering into a subway train door to try and make sense of its route map. And everything smells like wet cardboard. Trash floated on the historic Thames as we rode through it in the airport coach.

God knows how long Athena will wish to stay here. She breathlessly listed off about thirty things which are "absolute musts" in London. When we came in sight of Big Ben, she was waving her arms and crying, "There it is! Just exactly like it was in all those movies and pictures!"

"Were you afraid it wouldn't be there or would actually be only three feet high or something?" I said bitterly.

She didn't remark any more and I know she felt I was stealing the glamour of her first day in London. I admit that I cannot see anything glamorous in something like Big Ben that has been ogled by all kinds for ages and couldn't possibly be any surprise to her or anyone. The traffic is worse than I expected. I thought I would only be killed. I never thought seriously that the motorists would delight in my murder. They hurtle at you trying to gauge which way you will dodge so as not to miss you. You would think that there was a bounty paid on pedestrians. That the drivers cut notches in their bumpers to keep score of their victims.

I cough sporadically, my lungs singed by too many cigarettes. And each time I do, Athena gives a little start. This time she rolls over and tucks herself beside me. I look down at her. She is so tiny when curled up in sleep. So frail and dependent on me to keep her warm. How I wish her waking would not work its daily change on her. If she would only awaken today frightened and asking me to keep her safe, I could rise up and be a man to her.

But instead she will wake full of enthusiasm which will exaggerate my lack of same. She will be full of her plans and she will take charge of their implementation, leaving me to drag after. I fear the days are ending when she will remain satisfied that I am not in any traditional way a man. I sense her need for someone stronger than herself. I am beginning to think that I have been a pleasant oddity. He who said funny things and was so buffeted by life's winds that he needed sheltering. Now she might want repayment for that shelter. And, half of it being psychological shelter, she could never accept it from someone like me whom she believes to be psychologically weaker than herself. Why do people have to change? They come to me eager to prop me up, to give me a scaffolding that raises me above suffering. But what they give, they feel guiltless about taking back. No matter that I teeter and crash.

There are periodic thuds on the floor above me. Perhaps someone is being killed. And I lie here in this slightly damp bed, wishing only that they would finish their carpentry or homicide so that I could possibly trick my mind into sleep. My eyes refuse to close. I light another cigarette.

22: Travelling Has Always Been an Aid to Greater Maturity

Two weeks later, in a small upstairs room of a bed-and-breakfast house in Oxford, Athena and Tyrone lie clothed and abnormally far apart on the smallish double bed. Both have their knees up and their shoulders and heads propped up on their respective pillows. The room is trapezoidal and so small that the furniture clutters it and gives it the look of a storage closet. It is dimly lit from a single bulb hanging from a cord in the centre of the ceiling. The walls are papered. Vertical rows of pink and blue flowers set six inches apart. The paper is old and yellowing in places from the damp. Where the wall beneath the paper is uneven, there are ragged tears. Tyrone is pale and Athena's expression is grim. Her breath can be heard. She is breathing hard through her nose to emphasize her anger.

Athena – I don't see why it's so necessary for you to ruin every single thing we do! You won't let anything happen like it's supposed to happen. You always have to try and say the least appropriate thing you can think of. And it's not funny, Tyrone. It never is.

Tyrone – I was not trying to embarrass you or to be funny.

Athena – Then what in hell were you trying to do?

Tyrone – I was asking a simple question in order to find out a simple thing.

Athena – Oh. I suppose I'm supposed to believe that. That you really wanted to know if it was permissible to blow your nose in the college chapel.

Tyrone – I did.

Athena – Then why did you say it the way you did, "Is one allowed to blow one's nose in these hallowed confines?"

Tyrone – So he'd understand me.

Athena – Oh hell!

(There is a short silence in which Athena grabs a newspaper and pretends to read it. Then she throws it down again.)

Athena – I wouldn't be so upset if it was only today. But it's every bloody day! I only suggested we go to the college because I thought it would be something you would appreciate.

Tyrone – I was available. You could've asked me if I wanted to go.

Athena – We'd never get out of these rooms if we did what you say you want to do. Oh I'm sorry, except for the pubs. You're always eager to go and get drunk. Honestly, Tyrone, since you always say you won't like anything and everything, I have to guess at what you might like and drag you there. And you always make a fool of me.

Tyrone – It's all in your mind.

Athena – Oh is it? You tying the handkerchief around your face at the changing of the guard because you were afraid of germs. That didn't really happen? And, I suppose, I imagined that you yelled fire in the subway elevator. And it was all a dream that you put your fingers on the Rembrandt in the National Gallery and we were told to leave . . .

Tyrone – I have told you time and time again that an old man tripped me with his cane. You should be grateful that my finger didn't go through or that it didn't fall down off the wall.

Athena – And what about at the Tower of London? Was that an accident too?

Tyrone – (With little conviction.) That was just a joke.

Athena – Just a barrel of laughs. I almost died laughing when I saw you with the security guard's hat on, telling everyone, "Due to the great security risk, the jewels you have just paid twenty pence to see are all fakes." I noticed the guard laughing it up too as he escorted us outside and off the grounds.

(A long pause.)

Athena – (Staring across the room, mulling a difficult thought.) Just because you didn't want to come to Europe, you don't have to torment me for bringing you.

Tyrone – (Startled.) You knew . . .

Athena – Oh, of course I knew. You never seem to realize what an open book you are. Either that or you think everyone else is stupid.

Tyrone – But if you knew, why did you make me come?

Athena – For lots of reasons.

Tyrone – (Worked up.) If you knew so much, you should've known the whole trip would be a farce. Now why did you?

(Athena is silent. Sorry that she has gone this far, she wishes to go no farther.)

Tyrone – C'mon, tell me. God, do you have any idea how little I wanted to go?

Athena – I think I know exactly how little. You loathed the thought.

Tyrone – Then why!

(Athena stares at him, ashamed for them both.)

Athena – Because I thought it would make you into a man!

(Tyrone stands up, hands in pockets, walks down the room's tiny aisle.)

Athena – I am so sick, Tyrone, of you being afraid of anything and everything. All your bragging and pretending you were a big, bullying he-man. I saw through it from the start. I just thought that coming to Europe might force you to change. But I was wrong. You're worse than ever. You just want to cower in your room.

(A silence. Tyrone continues to stand. He would like to sit but feels suddenly that he has no right.)

Tyrone – Damn it, Athena! You could've saved all this armchair psychiatry and this stupid trip by asking me if a trip would change me. Nothing's going to change me. I mean, if it's so necessary that I be a man, you'd better go out and shop for one. I'm me, for god's sake! Not a piece of putty you can pull and push to your liking.

Athena – At first, I didn't think it mattered that you were scared of everything.

Tyrone – Say coward, it saves time.

Athena – I was sick of all those muscle men at college. You were so sweet and cuddly. It was so new to me I didn't mind the other stuff. But, lately, I don't know what's gotten into me. I keep thinking about marriage and kids and all those boring, reactionary things. And I couldn't marry a guy who was weaker than me. Do you understand me?

Tyrone – Yes, all right. I understand. Well, I guess that's all there is to it. Mind if I sit and go crazy for a while before I leave.

Athena – Don't be melodramatic, Tyrone! I don't want you to go anywhere.

(Tyrone sits bewildered.)

Tyrone – Hold on now. Let's try to set this in a bit of perspective. First, you don't like cowardice?

Athena – No.

Tyrone – You want someone strong?

Athena – Yes.

Tyrone – I am weak and a coward?

Athena – Yes.

Tyrone – Then you don't want me, right?

Athena – Wrong. I do want you. That's why we're here. It's because I want you.

Tyrone – Several thousand years of logic right down the drain.

Athena – You're not *only* a coward, Tyrone.

Tyrone – I am all coward.

Athena – No one's all any one thing! You're everything all the others weren't. Compassionate, thoughtful, introspective, sweet. But, you're not what they were either. The point is that what you are is much much rarer. It's just I'm greedy I guess. I want everything in a man. Including that he be a man! And that's why I want to try and make you a little more courageous. If I thought you were hopeless, I wouldn't bother.

Tyrone – I am what I am. Europe, Tasmania, or death aren't going to make Tyrone Lock a war hero.

Athena – You're so damned obstinate! It's in you to be as brave as anyone! I've seen glimpses of it. All that prevents it is your stupid idea that you're unchangeable.

Tyrone – Well, doctor, what do you prescribe?

Athena – I think we should separate for two weeks. If you haven't managed to come to some sort of terms with your terror of everything by then, I think we should call it all off. I'm sorry to have to say that, Tyrone, for me as well as for you. I'm sure I love you, but I'm too practical. If we got married with you like you are, it would be a shambles.

Tyrone – Why marriage all of a sudden, anyway?

Athena – I don't know why. I just want a husband and kids and a home of my own. The rest of mankind can get away with it without having trunks full of reasons.

Tyrone – Then we might as well call it off right now. You can't possibly expect me to become a father figure in two weeks. I wouldn't even know where to start. I'd make a lousy husband and I can't even imagine what I'd do to kids. I don't even like them.

Athena – That's what this whole therapy is designed for, Tyrone. I read about it in a course text for Social Psychology. When a person is forced into a strange environment where he or she must fend for him or herself and take charge of his or her responsibilities, he or she matures very rapidly.

Tyrone – That's ridiculous!

Athena – It isn't, Tyrone. You've always depended on someone. In

Canada, it was your parents and here it's me. That's why it isn't working so far. If you're here by yourself, something's bound to happen. I know it will work.

Tyrone – Athena, I don't want to change into a he-man. And I don't want to get married. I don't want to hold a responsible job.

Athena – You're so immature. Those are the facts of life. You should have recognized them years ago.

Tyrone – I didn't, and I'm not likely to in two weeks.

Athena – Do you love me?

Tyrone – (Maliciously.) Yes! *Athena* – Do you want me?

Tyrone – Yes.

Athena – Then you're going to have to. I've made up my mind and that's that.

(Later in the same room.)

I want a cigarette. Although my throat is lacerated and I am perpetually on the verge of coughing, my nerves demand one. I am not even granted the release of a good night's sleep. The unrelenting cruelty of life.

Where, I wonder, did the grand old concept of boundless love go? The passion that blinded people to earthly facts. Athena's love abandons the traditions of the past. Her love is the offspring of a scientific age. Its pragmatism excludes me. I do not compute. Therefore, subtract me.

A sad day when women's thoughts turn to marriage. They become so unsensuous. They rob man of sex, his only weapon against them. They fill their minds with washing machines and diaper pails and we are left helpless. Forced to share them with a horde of things as we become just one more item on the budget.

Why, Athena? Weren't you happy as you were? Couldn't you be satisfied to let us be no matter how poorly our futures matched? Isn't it fallacy to pay so much attention at a little passing time?

Everyone is so busy staring into books written by fools. Ostracize their infants because they haven't produced teeth at the mean age as computed by such and such. Horrified that little Harvey doesn't bother to journey to his potty to relieve himself when the expert says he ought to.

They are told by computers what to look for in a mate. Hunt him or her down as if they were shopping for beefsteak. Marry at the age some guidebook claims is best. And now my Athena divorces herself from all the beautiful realities we've shared. I suppose the night of glory when we met has been categorized as a such and such experience indicative of the following. Maybe men clutch at the past while women make demands on the future. Athena has decided that certain future items must be assured. In tune with her excitement over Big Ben, she craves the well-documented, the healthy, the normal things of adult life. Wishes to repeat what has been repeated many millions of times before. A safe and secure home; a completely planned family; a comfortable level of income, meaning probably astronomically high; life insurance; college investment for the kiddies; a set of encyclopedias that no one ever touches except to solve a stubborn crossword-puzzle clue; music lessons; a wooden plaque of the Last Supper.

And I do not fit her image of a husband. And rightly so, because I am the image of the worst one I can imagine. I may be able to draw her love, but what she would call her maturity says that rates a small score. Without an ability to fit into home movies, bouncing kiddies on my knee, or drying dishes, the love I can evoke must be unsatisfactory. So, I have been given a deadline of two weeks. If I had a colony of psychiatrists and plastic surgeons at my disposal, there would still be little hope.

And who is the coward, anyway? Doesn't Athena in wishing me brave and normal assure herself a future safe and secure from perversity? Don't I, in continuing to wander aimlessly, an emotional misfit, aspire to a certain bravery? No, I'm wrong here. I wouldn't choose to be abnormal if I knew how to be otherwise.

And who cares at this point what the causes are, or who is morally correct? To look at Athena asleep beside me after lovemaking, and to know it may be the last time, is to suffer several eternities of hell. I am so torn apart. Wouldn't really make a difference to the pain if her reasons were good ones. And this game that she has drawn up to end it all! Makes our love into such an unsanctimonious circus. She forces me to live a poor fairy tale. Invented by a social psychologist.

Athena, resting there so quietly against me, why did you have to be a psychology major at university? And why did you have to possess such a modern morality toward romantic matters? Why should all these facts and epigrams of naked theory overcome your love? Make it such a low-weight factor in some statistical compilation?

If only you were somehow from the nineteenth century! Then I, having your body and your love, would have all of you forever.

James Joyce declared the soul to own a virginity which is lost with the first wholesale giving of love. So, Athena, having once given her love to another, lord knows where or how long ago, takes from me now only a shadow of her real love. This thing so vapid and intangible, yet mortal. You cast it here and then, walking away, cast it there and no one can really keep it, for it is only a shadow.

But what of the virginity of my soul? What makes the shadow of my love so reluctant to leave her? Like a cartoon of a man walking in one direction as his silhouette walks in the other. Haven't I loved others? Don't I still love the ghosts of old girlfriends? Or does the definition of the term elude me? Joyce says simply, "To wish someone well." This is no help. His meaning is forever lost in the ambiguities of language.

I think my soul's virginity must be a composite thing. That I, in loving, give grudgingly. Saving something back in my endless fear of stolen gifts. So I gave a little chunk to the girl in junior high and suffered its loss when she tore my picture up before my eyes. And this piece of my soul lies with her yet. And the others got what love they asked for. It was not all, but it was all they wanted. And thus my love for them lives on and they pay their bit of rental in my heart. And now Athena, who asked more and received more and now takes more with her. And I will suffer.

How long until all my love is sucked out and my passion becomes only a bit of nostalgia? The rape of my soul complete? With nothing left of vivid passions to give, must I then become like Athena? Twisting people into unnatural shapes to discover the utmost in compatibility? Dissecting the psyches of my victims and comparing the pieces with textbook diagrams? And it is known as maturity. God spare me this fullness of life.

Another cold and clammy night. The air steals under the covers and murders our body heat. My limbs are cramped with cold. The odd vehicle roars by, shaking the windows with its trailing rush of air. Too remindful that tomorrow I will stand by myself on a bit of road begging favour from passing left-handed motorists. Going I care not where. Athena left behind me.

"Now, WE will meet again on the fifteenth of November in the cafeteria at the Museum of Natural History in London. Between three and four in the afternoon. Have you got it?"

"What if I'm late?"

"Then come back the next day at the same time. But, if this has worked at all, you should be responsible enough to be on time."

We stand on the street. Packs on our backs. Athena going one way, I the other. It is a thickly overcast day. Suitably dismal. Athena looks at me and for a few seconds her authoritarianism gives away to womanism. A little dampness around her eyes as she pushes onto tiptoes to kiss me briefly.

"Don't look so dismal, honey. Think how much better things will be afterwards."

I look at her, my pathos declaring my conviction that this entire idea is doomed and that our love is in its death throes.

"It will too work, Tyrone. I'm confident you can do it. Just give yourself a chance. Now take care, honey. I'll see you in two weeks."

She squeezes my hand and I can say nothing. Though she claims a higher ideal, the result will be the same. I am gone from her. She turns and walks rapidly away. Strutting almost. Wishing, no doubt, she could run. I stand frozen to these pavement footholds. Feeling the fibres of our union stretch tighter and tighter. Then snap, and I am stung hard by the recoil. I turn slowly and drag the wilted ends of my love away.

23: Cultural Differences Will Require on Your Part a Readiness To Compromise

I MUST admit it's pretty here, walking where I have been dropped off. The man who was driving me said the Bristol Channel is somewhere toward my right. He said I was also close to the home of the fictional "Hound of the Baskervilles." But I long to see nothing. I accept what I do see, but refuse to search anything out. Let alone go in search of moors full of mist and monster dogs.

Fairyland hills surround me, cut into squares of varying shades of green by dark rows of hedge. The leaves are still hanging on these trees in their bountiful reds and yellows. I've been treated to two falls this year. Didn't ask to be. Was willing to wait until next autumn to see another. A small price to pay for remaining in a less painful Canadian exile.

It has been four days since Oxford and Athena walked themselves from my life. Four drunken days in which I sought and found oblivion in lukewarm pints and pints of distasteful bitter. Nothing too eventful has happened. A few people asked me wheres and whys about my homeless presence. I told them incomplete truths and they said I was lucky. I told them I didn't feel lucky. And in particular states of drunkenness, I said a number of other things which no doubt put the national image in jeopardy.

I have stuffed money into one-armed bandits and lost myself gratefully in the blur of symbols. When money pops out, I seldom know why. Escape rather than avarice being my aim.

The nights have been endless tortures. I have spent them in flea-ridden hostels; aboard skinny bunks in dormitory rooms. My ears filled with the brutal night noises of other men. I have slept little. Only when the oceans of beer washed up over my consciousness.

And now I walk with little feeling for the automatic movements of my body. My mind far off in its torments. Trying helplessly to endow the days with some why. I do not hold my thumb out now, though the straps of my pack bite into my shoulders. I have no wish to travel today. It seems so unimportant where I waste the remaining time.

And as for the pitiful purpose of this Odyssey, I feel not an ounce less fearful, not a grain more marriageable. When someone stops to pick me up I am besieged by an urge to flag him on. In that second, all these good-hearted people take on the look of murderers, thieves, and sexual deviants. As we drive, I wince at their speed and nearly faint if they turn their heads to me to talk. I am afraid to breathe in any crowd. Afraid to eat the food I've ordered. I tremble when I hear a dog bark. I loathe the sight of children. Women wheeling prams full of rattle-wagging babies alarm me completely.

Where is the progress Athena promised? In fact, I feel deteriorated. I haven't shaved in these four days. Even now, I can smell my unclean self. I smoke recklessly. There seems now to be little purpose in self-preservation. Although each night of broken sleep is a torture of bad dreams, I cannot be bothered to rise in the mornings. Every movement is a burden. Lethargy dominates every facet of every day.

And now a man pulls over for me, uninvited. I climb in with a usual salutation. I tell the usual lies. He is an ordinary-looking person. His build is slim. His dress formal. His introductory chat is jailed in academic analysis. He looks at me often over wire-rimmed glasses. He is an artist. He tells me why he paints. My questions are uninspired and automatic. He is going to Penzance. I guess I am going there also. He is a tireless talker and I am grateful that I must only grunt. I find it relaxing and rock tensionless in the bucket seat as our journey continues. We stop somewhere and he buys me a pint. He asks me if I have somewhere to stay in Penzance. I tell him the youth hostel. He says it is closed. I say a bed-and-breakfast then. He says that I can stay at his house if I like. His girlfriend is away for the weekend. Also the other tenants are away. So I may stay. He must go out for dinner this evening but I can drink coffee and watch television. Go out for a drink as I see fit. He has painted a very homey picture. I can see myself in this comfort already and I say I will gladly.

Later, we sit in his house munching cookies and drinking coffee. I am very pleased at this lull in the storm. He talks endlessly of anything. He has thawed and is now even more glib. He makes me laugh. Something I haven't done in so long it surprises me each time I do. He seems pleased that I am so speechless. I am what he wanted. An ear to absorb his oratory.

And finally he comes out dressed for dinner. Says he will show me to my room. We climb the stairs and I deposit my pack in the indicated room. It confuses me. The decor is feminine. Pale yellow, silky sheets on the bed. Matching pillowcases with ruffles on the perimeter. The heavy scent of perfume on the air. But men's clothes lie about the floor. I take only small note of it all and we go back down. He leaves for his dinner party which he says he dreads.

I brew myself coffee and relax in front of the TV. Biscuits and cigarettes are all within easy reach. I am in a stolen ecstasy and marvel that this mercy has been granted to me.

As the evening progresses, I become more and more distracted by his paintings where they sit on the floor, leaning against the wall. I repeatedly glance from one to the other until the semicircle of them is completed. And each time I become less comfortable. Some are just black outlines of figures on blank backgrounds. The thick, sloppy lines capture naked men and women. Their sex exaggerated beyond purpose. No painting contains both men and women, and there is something about the figures that robs them of any spirit not sexual. The most disturbing of all is a depiction of crucifixion. The man on the cross is naked and thinly fleshed with torrents of blood gushing from the five tiny wounds. There is an X drawn on the crotch. I can't be recaptured by the TV drama. I am continually reviewing the paintings with growing unease. Slowly, reluctantly, I admit to myself that my host is a pervert.

I don't wish to see him again. I will go to bed, I think, and up the stairs I go. Into this strange bed, luxuriant with its spice box of odours.

I am tired from walking and the shortness of these recent nights. The familiar horrors of my mind are cut off by sleep.

FROM DREAMLESS darkness I am now suddenly torn. All around is a feeling of hideousness. Something is very wrong. The room is black and my mind is suffering to know its problem. I am quite awake now. And the bits of my attention focus on my ass upon which something rests. That something moves and I cry out.

"Ssh! What's the matter?" The voice of a man. His voice. Oh god!

"What's your hand doing on my ass?"

"Caressing it."

"Oh shit! Why are you here at all?"

"You forget, my little friend. This is my house. My bedroom. My bed. I quite regularly sleep in it."

It is the same voice but now touched up with lisping inflections. His bed. All becomes too clear. I roll over and there he is in silhouette, his head resting on his hand. His other hand gropes at me.

"Shit! Would you stop?"

"Relax, my friend. Why don't you rid yourself of that horrible garment. It's so interfering."

"Look, not meaning to be insulting but, I think I'll sleep on the floor or something."

"Don't be so stupid. You'd freeze on the floor. I should think it would be very cold. Mind if I cuddle up?"

His hairy parts touch my skin and I leap out of bed trembling.

"This is embarrassing you horribly, isn't it?"

"Yes! What about your girlfriend and all that?"

"Quite true. She's away for the weekend. But I simply loathe to sleep alone."

"Why didn't you ask or something?"

"I don't know. Would've taken some of the fun away. Come on. Get rid of that ridiculous underwear and climb in."

"I think I should leave. I don't like this."

"There always has to be a first time. This is the twentieth century, my friend. Although I prefer girls, boys are some comfort in a pinch. There is no sense sacrificing an entire night to sleep. Take refuge with me in compromise."

"I think I'm going."

He punches his pillow in anger.

"Oh phooey! I didn't think you'd be such a spoilsport."

"You could've asked. I would've gladly told you I was a spoilsport."

"I can't stand to sleep alone!" he wails, punching furiously at his pillow. He was so normal so few hours ago. "I promise not to touch you if you sleep with me. I'll sleep over here on the far side of the bed. See, with my back to you. Please."

As he pleads, I find a curious conversation going on in my mind. The wind lashes at the windows, bearing rain that crackles on the panes. I look at my luminous watch face and see it is two in the morning. No hope of finding other lodging this late. I look at the bed and the patch I've warmed is almost visible. Goose pimples rise along my length.

"Please," he says, and I wordlessly climb back. Trying to choose a posture giving little territory for attack. He coos in contentment and I think to myself, this is your doing, Athena. Bitterness rises up in me against her. Will this make me into a better man? Will the fact that I'm taking shelter in another man's bed make me more admirable as a father and husband?

"Shall we talk?" he coos.

"Shut up!" I curse and he mutters that I am ungrateful. Long after he snores I am awake and bitter.

24: Think Safety: Travel by Rail and Always Carry Traveller's Cheques

IT ISN'T like me to carry a feeling with me through sleep, but the next morning I am still bitter. What is the therapeutic value of having my ass diddled?

"Oh Tyrone, that was to reaffirm your physical manhood on which much of your mental transfiguration will be based. By feeling revulsed in the homosexual encounter, you have unwittingly cast your vote with the moral good of heterosexual human relationship. And thus, with the moral good of wife and family."

He drove me into town, his house being a mile or so out of Penzance. Little more was said. He seemed eager to get rid of me and I was as eager to be got rid of.

I sit in a seaside restaurant munching egg and chips. Sipping the inevitable cup of tea. The chat, the tiny smidgen I can translate, is about whether 'tis nobler to own a gas heater or an electric. The conversation, to make a bad pun, is getting heated. The waitress, a couple of hundred pounds of brute fat, took out her anger on my egg. Tossed it down in front of me with its yolk ruptured and bleeding all over my plate. There was the usual remark about my clear-tea perversion and I answered with my usual defensive shrug. What else is there to do? Say, the Orientals invented it and they drink it black. So there.

I sit here for hours and can feel the waitress's unkind eyes upon me. Feels some sense of propriety here and doesn't like the thought of anyone getting anything even space for nothing.

"Haven't you anything better to do than sit here?" I answer no and get up to go. I hoist the pack up on my back and leave.

There is no mercy in the world. Both sides of the sea, people delight in the torment of others. Ramble over us impersonally with the respect a truck driver has for the surface of the road. The endless avarice in the human intention. Extending their hands as if in friendship. Hah! How stupid I was to think his hospitality would be free of charge! Thought I would be delighted to join him in frolic, having been granted a night of free shelter. And the fat waitress who looked so apt to oink doesn't want my ass all over a seat in her empty restaurant. Should have to pay, she thinks. A penny to rent a berth on a toilet for another example. I sometimes sit and read there, protected by the engaged sign for hours. I have to admit that there are few things you can rent for an indefinite length of time for the price of a penny. Some day they will probably install an ejector system or have the door designed to fly open after five minutes. I'm always very disappointed to pay my penny and then sniff that someone has just been there. There are few things as disgusting as a warm toilet seat. (Just what this story needed: a scatological epigram.)

I walk to the train station. I have a great desire to leave Penzance.

"When's the next train?"

"To where?"

"To anywhere."

"What do you mean to anywhere? You must have some idea where you want to go."

"No, I don't want to go anywhere in particular."

"Then why don't you stay in Penzance?"

"Because I want to leave."

"I take it you don't like Penzance?"

"Sir, hundreds of people must come through here every day. Do they all have to give you an acceptable reason before you'll let them leave?"

"Of course not. I just gather from your tone of voice and what you've said that you would find any place in the British Isles preferable to Penzance."

"I am not trying to insult Penzance. I would just like to know when the next train leaves. If you tell me where it's going, I could decide whether I want to go there or not."

"Are you a Yankee?"

"I'm a Canadian."

"Oh!" and he grins. "We in England owe you fellows a lot. The Canadian lads stood by us through both wars and we're grateful."

"Sir, you owe me nothing. I'm one generation too late. But I would appreciate a little information."

"I'll give you a hint, lad. Never be afraid to accept what your country's earned. If the German lads had been a little more ready to accept what they earned in the first war, there wouldn't have been any second war. That's my opinion on the subject."

"Sir, that's a nice theory. I'll be sure and tell my mother. She's a Hun, you see."

"That's all right, son. She's probably a fine woman. It's the ones that stayed in Germany we have to worry about."

"Sir, the next train?"

"I always tell the missus that you young blokes could use a good war. In many respects, anyway. For example now, you come in here wanting to know when the next train to anywhere is. Now if you'd gone to war, you wouldn't be so eager to wander. You'd be damn appreciative of home and family."

"Sir, I don't want to still be here when the next one breaks out, so would you mind telling me when the train is."

"I really couldn't tell you."

"What?"

"No, I really couldn't. There's been a freight train derailment up the line and all services are shut down for the time being. You'll have to get a bus if you're really set on leaving. Or hitchhike. Britain's renowned for its easy hitchhiking. Lorries'll give you a lift more often than not."

"When will the derailment be fixed?"

"I can't tell you that either. Ordinarily, an hour or two. But the rail-maintenance crews are talking strike."

"They're on strike?"

"No, but they might be within the hour. Their chief complaint is the large number of derailments. Why don't you come back in a couple of hours and maybe I'll be able to tell you more."

"Can I check my pack in for the meantime?"

"Certainly. The baggage check is over there on your left. Bye for now."

I check my pack and leave. I go to the docks and stand looking at the sea. The ocean is good therapy for my bitterness. Its enormity fills my mind and at the same time leaves it comfortably empty. Tomb-like. I sit on a cement pier and its cold sends shivers up me. But I remain there and the time goes by. So nice to lose track of myself. It will almost be worth the pneumonia I may get from the damp sea wind and icy cement. No one is disturbing me or coming around to charge rent. It may just be that sanctuary has been found.

"Look at the bleedin' poet. Be nice if we had the kind of life where there's time to sit on your arse admirin' the sea."

I look up and see two whiskery men in grimy coveralls who've arrived to work on a freight boat down the dock. They see me staring at them and the reversal of situation annoys them. Feel that I am putting them in the zoo.

"Look mate, this is a commercial pier. Why don't you go down the way? They've got pretty green benches where you tourists can sit as long as you bleedin' well like. We've got work to do."

I get up and walk away in the indicated direction. I am herded like a pig. I find the little green benches filled with children. Pummelling each other and screaming. I could never achieve the desired tone of misery here. I look at my watch and am happy to see that two hours went by before I was discovered enjoying myself on the pier.

On to the railway station. There is a curious hush. All the doors are closed. I try them. They are locked. I stand for a while bewildered and finally from around a corner comes the man who told me nothing for hours.

"Is this teatime or something?"

He stands curiously at attention as if to salute at any second. "I presume you are speaking about the fact that the railway station is closed down."

"You may presume so. Why is it closed?"

"The railway-maintenance workers decided in favour of strike action a half an hour ago."

"So, are you closing down because you have no business?"

"That is not the reason. The reason is that because of the close union ties of all railway employees, we are all on strike in sympathy with the maintenance crews."

"Could I get my luggage?"

"Absolutely not! Not a door opens, not a wheel turns until the pay rise comes through."

"But what about my luggage?"

"Nothing can be done. If you would like to complain I will write down the address of the main office for you. We'd be delighted to have you complain."

"I want my luggage. How long will the strike last?"

"Because of the importance of the railway to the running of the national economy, it's usually only a matter of a day or so until we get what we want."

"Why did you let me check my pack in the first place?"

"I had to, of course. To not do so would've been against all labour relations decorum. Either we are on strike or we are at work. No fiddle-faddle in between. When we checked your pack in we were at work. Now we are on strike. It's a simple case of your being victimized by the corrupt and incompetent management of this railway. If they paid us better, you would have your pack right now."

I am walking down the crowded street. Packless. Trapped in Penzance. At the mercy of perverts. I go into a store and buy a flat tweed cap which, when pulled down just above my eyes makes me look fierce and stormy.

I go along looking for a bed-and-breakfast house. I find one. Ring the bell and a little old lady peers out of a peephole at me. I am glad she is little and old. Hope only that she has no sister to give me hallucinations of *Arsenic and Old Lace.*

"What do you want?"

"Bed and breakfast for one." She peers out suspiciously.

"Where's your luggage?"

I explain my predicament.

"A likely story, but as long as you pay in advance, I couldn't much care."

The door creaks open and I go to take a step inside. She stops me.

"Oh no you don't. Not a foot in this doorway until I see thirty bob. Or else you'll be giving me a sob story in the morning that you were robbed on the street by hooligans."

I produce the loot and she turns all smiles. From somewhere a voice, "What is it, Alice?"

"Just a customer, Harriet! You rest easy!" She shrieks. Then to me, "That's my sister. She's a bit deaf."

I am shown my room which may have once been a closet abandoned as too small. There had to be a sister, I think as I flop back on the bed.

I spend a long time staring at the walls of my little cage. Then drop off to sleep.

I AWAKE and my watch says ten o'clock. I am gripped by a sort of panic. Soon the bars will close. I tear out and down to the waterfront. I dash into the first pub I see and am almost skewered by a wayward dart as I enter. I shinny up a stool and order a pint, which I down immediately. I am angry with myself for sleeping so long. Setting the stage for another night of loneliness in crushing silence. I won't be naturally tired and haven't left myself time to become paralytically drunk. This requires emergency measures. Order up a double whisky and then order another while the first is still scalding me head to toe. The old man behind the bar slams it down for me. "Peculiar way to commit suicide, isn't it?"

"Mind your own business."

He shrugs and works down the bar to friendlier quarters. I begin to relax as my vision goes askew. There will be sleep.

Now back on the street. The cold piercing me through to the back. But drunk as I am, the fact that the night air is making me shiver becomes unimportant. I walk along for a block or two. I am quite lost. I kick a tin can down the street. It rattles along through the silence and part of me is hoping that it wakes up everyone in their warm beds. Where the hell am I? Street lights exuding clouds of amber. Rows of attached houses behind a few square feet of shrub-filled front yard. They all look like this. Street after street the same. No help in finding the one in which I am living tonight. Suddenly I am out of the amber light. This street stretches down into darkness. Shadows of houses either side. Makes me shiver. Perhaps I am frightened of the dark too now. I stop. On my right is an alley. Halfway down it, there is light from the next street. I stumble into it. Each step toward light, a step farther from danger. Said one astronaut to another.

Out of the dark hops a figure. I ignore him as terror courses through me. I go to step by him but he bars my way. Pushes me backwards. I turn to run. There are two behind me, closing in. Oh to be home in my warm bed with the wind howling at the windows. I turn to run at the better odds. There are now three on that side. Perhaps if I run at them very fast, I will break their tackles and live another day. I shout a Blackfoot slogan which I fancy might sound terrifying although it only means, "Is that so?"

"Honja! Honja!" I have a flat tweed cap in karate! Beware! I am rambling at them full speed, screaming. Next, I am lying on my back in the muddy leaves, my breath completely gone. My fearsome cap floats in a puddle beside me. I heave in panic to get air back into my lungs. I do not move. They are laughing.

"What the fuck we got here, the wild man of Borneo?"

I lie panting, unable to move, the damp oozing through my clothes.

"What do you want?" I really don't want to know.

"Well, chappy, we're the Pirates of Penzance and this here is our private alley. Anyone wanders down a private alley of ours, we usually rob him. You a Yank?"

"A Canadian."

"Same difference, eh mates? Bleedin' North Americans are all filthy with money. Let's see your wallet, Yank."

I hand it to him. They all crowd around to look into it. Someone strikes a match.

"What's this? One bleedin' quid? Yer going to have to do better than that, Yank. C'mon, mates, turn him inside out."

A crowd of them are on me, tearing at my pockets.

"What did yer find?" he asks.

"Another seventy new pence. Wouldn't you know we'd find ourselves a poor Yank?"

"Probably the only one in existence," another says.

They all stare at me with scorn for being so poor.

"He isn't poor. Probably has it all stashed away in his suitcase. Too bad you haven't a bird with you, Yank. Then we could play with her while you ran and got your wad. Well, mates, check him over some more. Get his watch if he's got nothing else."

They're on me again. Feeling me over like I was a retail cabbage. My watch is slid off and then a hand locates my money belt.

"Hey, lookee here! Lookee here! The bastard's got himself a money belt."

He rips it off and hands it to the leader.

"Well you suspicious Yank, you. Figured you might get pickpocketed if you kept it all in your wallet. That it?"

They all laugh and crowd around my money belt. I could possibly run now if I wasn't paralysed with fear.

"Ooo! Traveller's cheques. Hordes of 'em! Look at 'em all! You pasty-faced Yank! You weren't suffering much, were you?" He counts them aloud.

"Look at that signature. It'll take me about five minutes to learn to forge that." He looks down at me, shaking his head.

"You know, Yank, you're stupid. You could've made a tidy sum out of these for yourself if you'd've looked us up on your own."

"What do you mean?" They all laugh again.

"He don't know what I mean. Like I was telling you, mates. These Yankee blokes are proper stupid." He looks back at me. "If you'd've taken these to the black market yourself, you could've got maybe half the value for them. Then you run to the people what sold 'em to you and cry that you've been robbed. Give 'em your little receipt, fill out a form, and get them all back again. Meanwhile, you've made yourself a bundle. But you Yanks are too loaded to worry about making a little more, that's your trouble. So we, the Pirates of Penzance, is going to make it for you."

They start off down the alley. Stop and come back.

"We've decided to tie you up. That way we'll get a head start and be cashing your cheques before you'll be crying that they were stolen." They drag me to a power pole and one pulls a length of plastic string from his pocket. Some little creature inside me is outraged and to the horror of the fearful rest of me, kicks out and catches the one with the string in the crotch. I jump up and take a wild swing at another. He casually ducks and another grab me by the arms.

"Stupid bastard!" They heave in unison and I fly backwards. There is a dull thud and . . .

25: Do Not Be Embarrassed To Seek Medical Service Or To Solicit the Aid of Police in Times of Need

I CAN hear birds. I go to move and a pain shoots up the back of my head. It makes me want to vomit. I glance around with my eyes only and see that I am in a big hospital ward. It is breakfast time and everyone else sits bibbed and spooning food into themselves. One old fellow sees me awake and shouts, "Nurse! The young bloke is coming to himself!"

A chubby nurse walks up and smiles motheringly.

"How do you feel?"

"Half dead."

"You might, I suppose. You had a nasty clip on the back of the head. What kind of company did you get yourself into?"

"I was robbed."

"A pity. But these are terrible times. Should I call the police for you, so you can make a statement?" I nod. "Did they get all your money, duck?" I nod again. "It's terrible. Still, you shouldn't fret. The medical service is free."

"How did I get here?"

"You wandered in delirious and passed out in the reception area. Don't you remember?"

"No. How long will I be here?"

"Only a day or so, duck. There's a bit of a concussion. Nothing to worry about. You'll just have a big headache for a day or two."

She leaves and much later the police come. They say they will tell the traveller's cheque people. Have I got the receipt? No, it is in my pack which is checked in at the railway station because of the strike. The strike is over, they say. There is little they can do without the receipt. I give them the baggage check and they go. They return after about an hour to tell me that the pack, having been held by the railway for more than twenty-four hours, is subject to a fine. Have I got the price of the fine? No. A great discussion commences and I am told that that presents a difficulty. They really don't know how they are going to get the money to bail out my pack. Have I any ideas? I say that I paid bed and breakfast to two old sisters and didn't stay there for obvious reasons. They say they know the ones. One's a little deaf? Yes, that's right. They tear off, flushed with excitement.

I lie sick. My head a ball of fuzzy pain aggravated by this jigsaw puzzle. And everything seems so loose at the ends. Everything refusing to connect to everything else. I seem to be marooned. Cannot proceed on these destroyed roads. I am half asleep now from the many pills they have told me to swallow. The jagged edges are rounded off the pain. It feels as if the lump may be on someone else's head.

Some unknown time later, the policemen return. They look tired. The old ladies would not fork over. Said they rent beds and sell breakfasts. Immaterial to them whether the people sleep or eat. That's their business and making money is ours, she said. The policemen felt that she had a valid point concerning the tenancy of the bed, but questioned breakfast.

"I said to her, 'If he hasn't had his breakfast you aren't out a thing and it doesn't seem right he should pay for it.' And then the old bat, do you know what she did? Took two eggs, a rasher, and a few slices of bread and chucked them in the garbage can. She says, 'There! He's had his breakfast.'

"But don't fret, lad. We're not beaten yet. There's two angles to be played before the game's up. If we can convince the chief that it's necessary to the keeping of law and order and that it may lead us to solving the case, he may budget us the few shillings to get your pack out. Or we might get him to give us a warrant to get the receipt. You still wouldn't have your pack but you'd have the satisfaction of knowing we were on the track of the bleeders what clubbed you."

They leave again. A nurse comes in and feeds me. She is very pretty with her little white crown. She spoons foul-tasting gruel into me. Cooing that I shouldn't chew or move or my head will hurt. I'll be better soon, she says. And isn't it a shame that the streets aren't a safe place for people to walk? And she goes and leaves me lonelier than I was before. And jealous of everyone she feeds.

Everyone in the ward stares at me. Some talk to me. But I am too sour to answer. More pills come and I swallow them obediently. I do not complain that the big one is stuck in my chest. Soon after, I am very tired and sleep again.

26: Never Panic: Face Each Crisis Collectedly

THE NIGHT passed, I suppose. I slept from light to light so wouldn't know on my own authority.

The police have stopped the cashing of my traveller's cheques, but claim that it is like spitting in a forest fire. The villains will again succeed if they have any sense.

I am to be released from the hospital. I protest, lying that I am sick and in awful pain. And it is only a bit of a lie, the pain being real, but emotional in quality. The world stands outside this antiseptic haven. It stands outside the window, stark and angry. The day is rainy, and a fierce wind blows a mist up through the streets. Puts streaks across this window. I don't want to face the weather or that foreign smell, the days of waiting for the traveller's cheque people and their stupid questions. I don't want to face the railway people about my pack and I don't want to face Athena with my story of robbers and queers and total failure. Would much sooner spend life here in convalescence. Always convalescent, because my life will always be ill. Now the doctor is here. Does it hurt? Yes, very much. We will give you a bottle of painkillers when you go. When we put you back on the street. Now the nurse, the pretty smiler, comes. Says, are you better now? I say no, I may never be better, and she doesn't sympathize very much. She loves only the sick and the dying. When you are better, you become of little interest to her. Psychological ailments disgust her as a waste of important medical time.

I am climbing into my clothes now, which someone has taken and washed. For the sake of maintaining some standard of sanitation. I am weary already and want to climb back into my bed, number seven. So named by a little black number on a gold card up on the wall there. I wonder, do they refer to me as number seven? Tell number seven he's being busted back to civilian life. There will be a tiny ceremony to strip him of his bedpan. I wave bye-bye to the old men and the little boy who were my roommates. I envy them their illnesses. All except number ten, who sleeps all day except when screaming and will die shortly of a runaway cancer. Bye-bye, number ten. Bye-bye, sweet smiler. Looking into your eyes with a mouth full of gruel will always be one of my finest memories. Bye-bye, chubby nurse who informed me that my short stay here was gratis.

I am now on the street. Buzzing with honking cars. Flooded with people in mad search of the ever-evasive bargain. And I suddenly wonder what day it is. Cannot even afford a paper to check. Find the office of the people who sell traveller's cheques. Walk in and up to a dapper man who is smiling widely.

"I am Tyrone Lock."

"Good. I am Harry Howard. What do you want?"

"You have the receipt for my traveller's cheques. The police brought it to you. I was robbed."

"Oh yes. How did it happen?"

I tell the story in gory detail. Dapper little man is looking at me with cynical distrust.

"It's an offence to make a false statement about the loss of your cheques, you know."

"I am telling the truth."

"Well, I only hope so. Write all of it down on this form."

I do and hand it back. There will be a delay. What am I to do without any money?

"That, I am afraid, is your problem," he says. "There is an unavoidable delay of two days. Come back then." Oh shit, I say.

Back on the street. My stomach rumbles although I was fed breakfast in the hospital. I am hungry with fear of being really hungry. How am I to survive two days without money? Who will give me back my hope? Back to my gay friend, hoping to be safe in the shadow of his returned girlfriend? Athena would no doubt be tickled pink with my predicament. Would say, there Tyrone, now you must certainly become big and strong and self-sufficient. While you sit shivering in a back alley in the falling rain you will learn to be responsible. Perhaps I could go to some religious order and say I would like to join up. Recruit and be fed by the Franciscans for two days, at which time I would abruptly lose my vocation. Or perhaps I could sell blood at the risk of transfusion hepatitis. Beg on the streets. Slam my finger in a door until it breaks and then go back to the hospital. Is there no painless option?

Now I stand at that little chunk of beach where the green benches stand. No children. All in school. Where they should be kept during all their waking hours. I sit on this little bench. Totally immobile for fear of green splinters in the ass. Which wouldn't stop until they got to my heart. Staring at the windy ocean. My hair slicked back by the breeze exposing that little spot of baldness I am so self-conscious about. Seems to be growing but never gets any bigger.

And what in hell will I do with myself? Hungry with no place to sleep. And don't anyone say, now you know how all the poor and starving feel. Because, of course, I do not. The poor and the hungry facing two days of shelterlessness and hunger would not be much bothered. If they were going to receive my reward at the end, they would be delighted. So, I will suffer more. And I am not willing.

I haven't shaved since Athena strutted away from the sunset into a rush-hour hodge-podge. I told the nurse I was growing a beard. Perhaps I will. A scrawny beard with weak spots. Some might take me for a slightly aging intellectual. I would never wash my hair, and comb it in such a way as to expose my erratically shaped bald spot. All to complete the image.

"There he is, lost in philosophy. Far removed from his stinking body. How romantic."

No one would know that my physical deterioration stems from something as paltry and prosaic as love lost.

Athena, I don't want to lose you! Even with your idiotic plans for my psychological welfare, and your will to heap a crowd of squalling babies between us. Even with all that, I would hate to lose you.

Hurry up now, ocean. Flood my mind and kick out the little anguishes that are building shacks there. All the homeless despairs of this world flock to me. Bang on my mind's door and then sneak in a window when my cautions are down. Then, suddenly, interrupting my contemplation of the hopelessness of things, my policemen friends are with me.

"You're looking much improved, lad."

"I feel worse."

"We've had no luck catching up with those fiddlers. Lucky for you, you were keeping traveller's cheques so that you're not out much."

Ha. Lot of good they will do me when I am lying frozen and quite dead in someone's coal shed.

"What sort of crime would you punish with a two-day jail sentence?"

"We never have any that short. You pay a fine for as minor an offence as that."

"If the culprit couldn't pay the fine, then you'd have to put him in jail. What sort of crime?"

"Drunk and disorderly. Breaking a small window. Things like that."

"Where's the nearest two-day-jail-sentence window?"

"Joseph," he says to the other, "I think that belt on the head has addled the poor lad's brain."

Joseph nods and they prepare to go.

"You've got to stick me in jail for the two days that it'll take to get my traveller's cheques back. I'll freeze to death otherwise. Please?"

"Oh, I see . . . No, don't go breaking any windows, lad. You'd be in for a damn lot longer than two days. Wouldn't he, Joseph?"

"But you said . . ."

"I know, lad. But that's only the jail sentence. You'd be in for a week before court convened. That's with no one to post your bail. And then you being a non-national, you'd most likely be pelted out of the country. No, you're all right. Better not do that, lad."

"Couldn't you just stick me in jail for two days anyway? No one would notice."

"The taxpayers would. They get very angry about the money they pay keeping the criminals in. Let alone if we start putting in people who haven't committed crimes."

"Protection then!"

"What're you shouting about now, lad?"

"I demand protection from the fellows that robbed me. I demand to be put in jail for my own good."

"That's no good either, lad. The superintendent knows that they're probably miles away by now. Besides, they know better than anyone that you haven't a bean left. You're not in a speck of danger."

And they go away. There is no hope apparently.

I have no cigarettes and have begun to shake. My bloodstream screams for its daily quota of pollution. The day drags on. I sit here and then there, very smilingly. In hopes that someone will come to chat and find out my unfortunate story. Saying, ah, won't you come home and be fed and housed? But no one comes, not even a single pervert. I'm feeling very hopeless and helpless as if time has chosen to stand still while my metabolism dwindles.

I go to the railway station, saying I only want my sleeping bag. You can keep the rest as insurance. He says, no dice. Must pay your fine. I say, you wouldn't have had any of it if it hadn't been for your stupid strike. He says, strikes aren't stupid, and is further hardened to my plight. I say he has no right to count the hours that the strike was on as time when the pack was held. He says, you may have a point there; why don't you write a letter? Then counts on his fingers to prove that even with the strike time subtracted, my pack has been in their custody for more that twenty-four hours. I shout, that's not the point! Write a letter then. Everyone's excuse for everything is to say, 'It isn't up to me. I don't make the rules. I haven't the authority. Write a letter.'

"What good will not giving me my sleeping bag do? If I freeze to death in the night, it will be on your conscience. And if you don't happen to have one of those, you still won't get your fine. So why not give me my sleeping bag?"

He stands fingering his jaw. Now bites one finger. Sticks the wet finger in his ear and digs around. Sniffs loudly twice. I think he might've forgotten I'm here.

"You may take your sleeping bag but the Lord help you if anyone finds out I let you have it."

No, sir, I will do nothing but be grateful. You noble bastard. He hands me the sleeping bag and I have the consolation of knowing I will only half freeze to death now.

A new thought comes into my mind. If I could sell my sleeping bag for even half its price, I could eat and sleep for two days. So I am off to the youth hostel, which I have been told is now open. I arrive at where it is hidden in the bushes so as to keep the youth of today a bit off the streets. I knock on its doors and there is an echo of emptiness. A little sign reminds me that it is closed midday until five. Curse it then. I will wait. It is now three. I sit on the cold cement veranda and the frost nibbles at my ass. All the better to develop haemorrhoids. I sit and sit and am slowly freezing to death. My heart is erratic with desire for nicotine. I itch all over, partly from dirtiness, mostly from nervousness. My beard is itching. So is my head. My mouth is filled with a foul gumminess. My teeth are furry and unbrushed. I am ever so slightly frantic and losing my mind. I pick my nose for company. Flick snot at various targets to remain amused. I wait and wait and eventually can wait no longer.

I walk down the street to where it empties out onto a beach. Look at the fishing vessels coming and going. Can see a coast guard ship sticking small out of the fuzzy horizon. Here an old freighter stands in dry dock, looking naked and abandoned. Like I feel. My stomach is convoluting like an eel. Screaming, feed me! And I feel quite sorry for myself. Forced to envy everyone. I loathe the little bumpkin who savages a chocolate bar before me. Count your lucky stars, bumpkin. Soon I will be chewing my boot leather like the perishing shipwrecked wanderers of centuries past. Now it is five and I must peddle my wares.

"Down-filled sleeping bag with waterproof nylon zipper, just like new because it is, a bargain at ten pounds. Unslept-in by human body. Good to sub-zero temperatures. Alive alive-o."

I step in the hostel door and canvass its customers. None seem to want a sleeping bag. My price is down to eight pounds. Soon seven pounds. Won't go a penny below five. Does little good, this price cutting. Everyone already has one. Affluent bastards. I race downtown panicky now. Don't want to sleep in the damp and cold. Wake up arthritic as a man of ninety. The shops are trying to close. Into a camping goods store. How much for this lovely sleeping bag? You don't buy or sell second-hand. Who does? Three blocks over, Tiverton's. Buys and sells anything. I run as if there was a mouse in my pants. Mr. Tiverton, hairy-faced, toothless beast that he is, is trying to lock the door. I bang on it.

"I'm closed!" he shouts through the glass.

I club away relentlessly. I will not sleep in the cold to save you five minutes, you old sod. He jerks open the door.

"Er you deaf? I'se closed," he growls. He spits and has bad breath.

"I'm willing to sell this sleeping bag very cheap."

"I'm not willing to buy it." I stick my foot in his door and he practically breaks it off.

"Five pounds! Only five pounds!"

"Three!"

"Four!"

"Two pound fifty."

"All right, all right!"

I walk away. My pretty forty-dollar sleeping bag gone for a pitiful two and a half pounds. Still, I will stay in the hostel these two nights and have one pound seventy pence to eat and smoke with. I confess to being relieved. And won't Athena be thrilled that I coped with my problem so smartly. The psychology faculty of the university will be delighted. Next we will teach him to jump through a burning ring. I wish I could eat, smoke, and get drunk on one pound seventy pence. I will fix up a budget for myself and see if I can work it all in.

27: Don't Miss the Warming Fire and the Lively Chat in a Typical English Pub

In front of this fire that licks in a sharp draft. With its glowing red heart, so cheery and frightening all at once. I stare into it. My face burns as my ass freezes. The good and bad of a fire. I am so pleased to be so bored. Nice when things get so back to normal that there is time for being bored silly.

Figures ticking off in my mind. Fifteen pence for breakfast times two is thirty. Thirty for dinner tomorrow. Two twenty-pence suppers is forty. Add them up and it makes one pound. Then there were those two chocolate bars I devoured after supper tonight. A pound eight pence. Thirty pence for that pack of cigarettes which I'll make last. Matches for one and a half makes a total of one pound thirty-nine and one-half. Leaving me thirty and one-half pence. Which will not get me drunk. Doesn't seem as important now as it did. Suffering for a change in the present tense plugged some of the holes where self-pity had formerly entered. Puts the Athena-derived pains into a bit of perspective. There is a great relief now in knowing that frostbite and death from exposure have diminished from probable to possible. And all that relief fogs the bit of perceptive glass that would ordinarily be focused on the loss of Athena. Perhaps this is the rationality everyone's been urging me to learn.

"Tyrone, by forcing yourself to always jump the fiery hurdle, full of desire to be safely on the other side, you deprive yourself of the time to feel the pain of being alive," said the psychologist to the depressive.

If hopefulness hadn't been an ingredient in the reasoning mind of man, we would have suicided ourselves to extinction in a past geological age. But no, there was always that hope, making us want to plug on and survive. To be for another day. When possibly all shit will alchemize to ice cream, and noses won't run, and cancer cells will learn to destroy themselves, and babies will only happen when absolutely wanted, and gums won't rot, and somebody who doesn't particularly want to live will die every time someone is born, and cowards will be given recognition like Red China; and Athena won't want to get married or at least would just as soon save baby-having for a future rainy day; and there wouldn't be any rainy days.

Tyrone, old friend and trusty admirer, would you care to join me for a pint of bitter in a nearby pub? We will reminisce about all our old successes and if they won't take up the space of one pint, we will simply not think during that time. We will take up the example of the old regulars who bow over their pints, always unaccompanied. We will stare into the glass as if a grand and glorious entertainment was going on there. But all forms of failure will be barred at the mind's doors and kept from the stage. Only the film stars of old in their most ego-enhancing roles will play for us tonight. Take my arm, Tyrone, and we will be off.

28: Always Be Courteous to Your Fellow Travellers

THE REGULAR click of tracks passed over. Like a throaty voice repeating an obscenity with the intention of driving us all mad. It is freezing cold on board this train and whenever my teeth come close together they chatter. The conductor is blaming it on the derailment. Claiming in the British tradition that he cannot help it. It's not his fault. After all he's just a conductor. Why don't you write a letter, the British answer to everything.

A mammoth of a woman, wearing a ridiculous flowered hat as if to disguise herself as a hilltop, jabs an elbow into her spidery husband at regular intervals, shouting, "Bloody hell, Terence, my feet are falling off!" He whispers back. No doubt advising her to write a letter.

Across the table from me sits a girl who is almost pretty. She has her hair drawn back viciously from her forehead and I imagine it is this alone that prevents her from being completely pretty. I have stared at her for perhaps fifty miles. She is anaesthetizing herself to the cold by ploughing her attentions into a woman's magazine. Once in a long while, she looks up, and I become suddenly interested in the panelling over her shoulder. She is my anaesthetic. Keeps me from both the cold and images of an angry Athena. Who will surely shout and drive me finally away tomorrow.

Oh, girl of the drawn-back hair. Would a little reassuring smile be too much to ask? Just a little smirk? It would save me the mental struggle of fantasizing our romantic moment. Would postpone my inevitable trip to the bar to pour beer on my sorrows.

The brakes screech and we slow into a station. The first sign flashes by. Rugby. My lady of the drawn-back hair goes into an instant frenzy. Stuffs things into her giant purse and climbs into her coat. Now she stands and tugs at her suitcase. It remains on the rack, unbudged. A gentleman to the rescue, I stand and offer to assist.

"I can do it myself!" She give a mighty heave and the suitcase comes free. Its corner smacks me a nasty one in the eye. She disappears out the door in a huff. I sit fingering my eye, which is beginning to swell. There is a fine line apparently between chivalry and chauvinism.

As our lady of absolute independence disappears, a scrawny woman comes in screeching instructions at a fat, cruel-looking child whom she guides toward me with little shoves.

"Do you mind if we sit here?" she shrieks. I shake my head, thinking, fine, sit on my face if you like. The fat child stares at me, evil in his eye. I duck as the woman rips the window open. Shoves her face out. Bellows, "Farewell, Bobby, my son. I'll take good care of Benjamin." We are about three hundred yards from the station now and the wind blasts at her voice. Bobby would have to have ears like an elephant to hear. Woman sits. Smothers Benjamin with affection.

"Nanny will take good care of Benjykins, won't she?"

"I want my car that makes a big noise!"

"Yes, my little darling."

Benjykins is given his little car which is as big as a loaf of bread. He makes big noises all over the table. I reach for my cigarettes and Benjykins shouts vroom, vroom, and races his machine over my hand. Stares at me with provocation. I am provoked. Little bastard. Why don't you take your nice car and your nice little self and go swimming in the toilet. I will be along shortly to flush.

I am off to the bar car which is a mile of cars away. I order four of anything and decide that selecting beer with care is an affectation of those who drink for enjoyment. I drink for escape.

Hoping for further distraction, I sit across from a suntanned lady. Her neck bows with jewellery. Her neckline swoops to expose things. Her hair is caught up in a kerchief. I stare at her hungrily as I consume. She ignores me without effort.

Then down sits a man in styled hair, sports jacket, and roll-neck.

Plants his arm possessively on her chair back. They begin nasal chit-chat. Talk of the sunny south of Spain where they have just holidayed. Explaining the suntan in this climate devoid of sun. They force me into my little world so packed with horror. Fiery-eyed goddess Athena shouts down at me from a height. Failure! Failure! Coward! Less than quarter of a man! All true. I have been a hopeless failure. Nothing to tell but failure and cowardice reinforced by lousy experiences. It's the fourteenth, and time marches me into London tomorrow. Into the Museum of Natural History.

I have only one opportunity to lie my way to a reprieve. But is there any use? Athena is on to me. Will be sleuthing through my every word for inexactitudes. How can I shove the necessary fairy tales past those scrutinizing eyes? I could polish my shoes and lower my voice and say between puffs on a smelly pipe, "My trip? Quite a success really. Climbed a few of their so-called mountains. Ran out of time, damn the luck, and didn't get a chance to take a trot up Ben Nevis. Went swimming off the coast of Wales. A touch cold and a few sharks but quite refreshing. Was I scared? Silly question, my dear. I am never scared. To be frightened in the face of danger is to face that danger with less than the utmost presence of mind. Had to harpoon a shark, in fact. Poor devil. But it was either him or my leg."

It's no use! I guzzle away at my beer. In a frenzy. What can I do? Tell the truth! It's all I really have. Perhaps if I twist the facts slightly.

"Oh, my trip? Not bad, I guess. I ran into a few problems. I was robbed in Penzance by a bunch of guys in an alley. Kicked one of them but there were too many for me. Was I hurt? Just a little concussion. I was over it in a day or two. It was a little tough for a couple of days after that until I could get my traveller's cheques back. But I sold my sleeping bag and as you can see, I survived."

I repeat this to myself. Do my ears deceive me? That sounded curiously like two things: the truth and exactly what the psychology department would like to hear. Two more beers and it sounds even better. Brilliant use of understatement, Tyrone. I pat myself on the back. Rehearse for the seventieth time. I am quite drunk and in a very celebrative mood now. I have won. My belief in happy endings is renewed. I am renewed. Athena will embrace me. Saying, I knew it would work. The final accent on the perfect deception will be to play at ignorance of my metamorphosis. And I will not have to deal with the loss of Athena. She will be so convinced, I can be as I am. She will interpret all my actions in terms of the change she thinks I have gone through and my continuing cowardice will be masked.

I am so elated that I start up a conversation with those who holiday in the south of Spain. They are sad to be returning to London after such a delightful time. It was all so thrilling and champion. The proprietary pissant turns out to be also a smart-assed Cambridge graduate. He fancies himself quite knowledgeable on the subject of Canada. Thinks our prime minister has just the flamboyance that the age needs. Says other things which display a similar ignorance. Drawing on the small array of facts I collected whilst being temporarily devoted to politics, I refute him. Then launch myself into a monologue on the good of my homeland. Am suddenly a raving nationalist. The last land of golden opportunity. Privacy attainable by means other than high brick walls. Where violence is still shocking. Where eccentricity is tolerated if not accepted.

The smart-assed Cambridge graduate says, why did you leave if you liked it so much? I answer that it was only to please a lady, and conversation stops abruptly. The chasm that separates the adventurer from the coward yawns as wide as ever.

But, if they are suddenly uncomfortable, I am not. Too glad and drunk to be bothered. For I will please my lady at long last. And then nothing but happy-ever-afters.

I look around. Starchy old fools. Sitting unnaturally straight. Bellies hanging over their belts. Burping politely behind the hand. Pretending that the hand is there to smooth out the moustaches. Down with pretence! And I issue a sonorous belch. Those that holiday in the sunny south of Spain stand and leave. May your thesis be universally condemned as humbug. No one takes the empty seats. Sooner stand hanging onto the railings, sloshing drink on themselves, than sit beside one who belches without the moustache-smoothing hand.

Why aren't any of you singing? Instead of boring each other with low-key conversation issuing from the nose? I sing a snatch of "In the Blue Canadian Rockies." Byrds-style. Several people stare nastily.

Bartender cranes his neck out and wags a finger. Points to a sign above himself. *Positively No Singing.*

Of course, Should've known you wouldn't be able to sing. Why, if people sang, the next thing they might laugh, and then what? Anything could happen. They might stop being so bored. Acquire new interests. And then what? Communism and all sorts of un-British things. The economy would collapse.

I am a bit drunk, I think. I stand up and totter to the left and then to the right. Maybe more than a bit. Gain the first door. Plummet down the aisle beside a row of first-class compartments. Glimpses of fat people asleep, heads resting on white hankies. Now through another car. Rollicking from side to side. Miss a seat top and balance myself for a second using someone's head. Sorry about that. A few more chaotic cars and I slump down across from Benjykins and Nanny.

"I am going to sleep! If you so much as touch me, Benjamin, I am going to throw you and your car that makes a big noise right out the window."

"Well, I never . . ."

"Goes for you too, nanny." Eyes slam shut.

29: Last But Not Least: Have Fun and Come Home Safely

WALKING AMONG stuffed animals. Fish floating in the air on strings. The skeleton of the last survivor of the sea cows sits on a stand. God rest her race.

It most certainly is the fifteenth.

I walk along. Now in the science museum. The history of technology before me. I am early. Wallowing in responsibility. I shove a penny in a glass case and watch a wheel with little buckets raise water and dump it down a slide. In the distance, a thousand clocks tick. Onward, Tyrone, to the cafeteria. All is going to turn out fine.

With your terrific plan nothing can go wrong. Then why am I so worried? Why does my heart threaten to stop with every step? It sounded so foolproof last night. When I was drunk.

On the elevator. Rising above a row of vintage cars. Off one elevator, onto another. Five minutes to three. Two more elevators. Cafeteria this way. Through the section devoted to the movement of celestial bodies. I look at old telescopes in a desperation of procrastination. What a nice sundial. The whole building has conspired to remind me that time has run out. I feel as if I stand in a giant hourglass up to my neck in sand. As it relentlessly pours down.

In the cafeteria now. No Athena. No anyone except the peculiar little man with the massive head of hair who works here. A giant forelock bobs down over his face as he walks. I sit with my coffee. Light a cigarette from the butt of my last one. Madly puffing a smoke halo around myself. The little man is peering at me from beneath his forelock. Fiercely. Another pervert, I suppose. Where in hell is Athena? The woman's prerogative as she calls it. To build up the suspense to freaky heights. Fulfilling her dreams of Hollywood romance. No wonder they live longer.

This tense appointment is such a far cry from that golden night in Sally's sixth room. Still, I have missed Athena. Some part of me will be jumping with emotion when she comes. My cigarette is gone. Also the coffee. Light another. Buy another. Why is this man peering at me? The great urge is to make a face.

"Say, mate, you wouldn't be waiting for a bird, would you? Tall, blonde, beautiful."

I nod, nod, and nod. All the clocks in my world have stopped. The grains of sand refuse to fall.

"Well, she left you a note, mate. I wish I had a pretty bird like that dropping letters after me. But I'm not what you might call a lady's man. Anyway, you hold on a minute and I'll fetch it. Would've picked you out sooner, but the bird said you'd most likely not be here until four."

He hands me the letter. I sit in a great hush and look on the envelope. Air Mail scratched out. She is so niggling about the tiny detail. But my name is made regal by her elegant hand. I shake a little as I split the seam.

> Dear Tyrone,
>
> I don't care how insincere it sounds, I'm going to start off by saying I'm sorry anyway. I'm sorry among other things for not having the guts to meet you in person. I guess that proves who was the coward after all.
>
> Please believe me, Tyrone, when I say that I sent you away for those two weeks in good faith. I meant everything I said about wanting you and thinking that the two weeks would help you. I didn't know then that I'd meet Cliff. He's so wonderful, Tyrone. He's quite a bit like you, in fact, but we make a much better pair. I think we'll be married soon.

So that limits how sorry I can really be, doesn't it? Because I honestly believe it's the best thing that could've happened for both our sakes.

I can see now that you were right. You couldn't change in two weeks. I was wrong to expect it and to force you to do so many things you didn't want to do. Try to forgive me, Tyrone.

I'll never forget you. I don't think anyone really could forget you who has known you well. I hope you meet the person you need, some day. I wish you happiness.

Love,
Athena

In a banging subway. Hurtling into black. Squeezed between people larger than he. Sits our hero. The corner of a *Guardian* fluttering in his face. Inducing not one blink.

As I stare out the black window at parallel pipes whizzing by. Flipping in and out of white-tiled platforms full of quiet hordes. Politely pushing. I read the names on the blue bars at each pause. Victoria. South Kensington. Earl's Court Road. Leading me. Where? Some place called Uxbridge. Where I will turn around and come back.

What's going on in my mind? Not much really. Pictures mostly. Mountains and cows. An old house disappearing in snow. A tall, blonde girl with a pack on, walking away down a street. A letter with my name on it and the airmail stamp scratched out. And a funny, lost-looking guy with a lot of shaving pimples, coming out of a museum. I guess that's me.

Afterword

To READ *Lonesome Hero*, my first novel, a novel I wrote over thirty years ago, feels odd. So much time has passed – the difference between a twenty-year-old and a fifty-something – that it is easier for me to identify with the parents and the community elders than with the young protagonist, Tyrone. To some extent, that has to be a good thing. If I was still exactly the same person who wrote *Lonesome Hero*, it would signify a serious failure to progress. But, if the book blocks me at first, persistence is rewarded. Eventually, I am able to become both Tyrone and the fellow who created him, and for this among other reasons, I am glad I wrote it. Who wouldn't want a means of being twenty again, thirty years after the fact?

I wrote this novel while in England, Ireland, Holland, France, and Spain. Nowadays, that might suggest that I came from a well-to-do background, but actually it had more to do with the relative cheapness of travel in 1972. I was the son of southern Alberta farmers and a recent graduate of the University of Calgary. I had saved the money for the trip by living frugally and saving carefully from my summer wages on turn-around crews at sour gas plants.

I left Canada a month after Team Canada's marginal victory over the Russians in the original Summit series, which is to say I saw Paul Henderson score that famous goal when it happened. Thanks to CBC milking the event for nationalist significance ever since, I've seen it at least a thousand times and hope never to see it again. The time of my departure was also a month after the massacre of Jewish athletes at the Munich Olympics, and shortly before the federal election of October 31st that saw the Trudeau Liberals returned to power, two seats short of a majority. While I was away, Lester B. Pearson died, and the United States continued to bomb North Vietnam.

It was a time in history when I and most of my friends were letting our hair grow and hoping never to work in an office. To never work at all was the ultimate hope. At university, I had studied Economics, for the shrewd reason that it was the major of my roommate Bryan and would save me money on books. My heroes were Leonard Cohen, J. P. Donleavy, Jimi Hendrix, Joni Mitchell, Jean Beliveau, Neil Young, Mordecai Richler, Gordon Lightfoot, and Led Zeppelin, in no particular order. It was late enough in the Age of Aquarius that some of us had begun to experiment with not taking drugs. For some time, my two ambitions had been to spend a year in Europe and to write a novel, and, suddenly, I was doing both.

I wrote this novel in the first three months of my journey, while riding trains and hitching rides, and staying in youth hostels and bug-ridden hotels. According to letters home, I had time as well to see the sights and have adventures. I remember being chased off an island in Lake Windermere by a pack of enraged wolf hounds. In my panic, I failed to navigate a turn in the path and ran off a fifteen-foot cliff. I remember being fleeced in Dublin by a con man who claimed to be from Moose Jaw. (If he happens to be reading this, I still want my hundred bucks back!) Some of Tyrone's adventures in Britain were my own.

As for the novel, there was a deadline involved. I was trying to enter the first Search-For-An-Alberta-Novelist Competition, put on by the Literary Arts Branch of Alberta's Department of Culture. The deadline was in February and I had to write very quickly. For the first time, I experienced that heady "story writing itself" feeling: a headlong, exciting, plunge toward an unknown destination. People have told me that they wept at the ending of *Lonesome Hero*. So did I. And I did make it in time for the contest deadline, but with more help from my family and a family friend than was ever fair to request.

The novel was written in many scribblers, which I hauled along in my backpack. I thought I would stumble on a typewriter somewhere along the line. But it did not happen. With a great lump in my throat, I sent the bundle of scribblers home, with a pathetic note asking my family to hire someone to type it. But I knew right then that they would try to do it themselves.

Let me take this opportunity to thank my older sisters, Marie and Lois, for the work they did typing *Lonesome Hero* into a manuscript. Thanks as well to Joyce McFarland, from two miles down the road, who also did a great deal of the work out of simple good-heartedness and good-neighbourliness. Joyce had lived in cities and worked as a professional secretary before marrying a local bachelor, and I have often winced at the thought of her typing away on my novel that was so often sarcastic about a farm community not unlike our own. Later, in her assertive way, Joyce would tell me she thought it was a good book. There was something in her tone that said, "and let the chips fall where they may."

Thanks to this typing bee, the novel made it to Edmonton by the contest deadline.

At this point, the story enters a hiatus. The novel went to its impressive panel of judges: Edmonton professor and novelist George Hardy, long-time University of Alberta president Walter Johns, and publisher and writer Lovat Dickson (the amazing man who introduced Grey Owl to the British). Meanwhile, I was continuing to travel, including my first experience of Greece. It was not Greece's finest hour, given the ugly crackdowns by the US-backed Papadopoulos junta, but from the perspective of the honeycombed cliffs of southern Crete, it was hard to feel anything but blissed out. Running low on money, I worked for a time in a beautiful old hotel on the island of Hydra: Leonard Cohen's Hydra, referred to in many of his poems and songs.

When the news came that my novel was one of two finalists in the competition and had been chosen for publication by Macmillan of Canada, I was in Germany, staying with my mother's relatives. They ran the village bakery, and when a cousin came to the back to tell me I had an overseas call, I was scrubbing cooking sheets and cake pans.

Phoning me in Europe was an uncharacteristic extravagance for my family, and I assumed when I heard my mother's voice that something awful had occurred.

The news about the novel was conveyed, the phone call ended, and I started running around the bakery jumping for joy. There was not a lot of lingo in common between my relatives and me, and who knows what I managed to tell them: perhaps that I had written a very long poem for which the government was planning to kill me. (For the record, *Bird at the Window* by Jan Truss won the competition, and the other published finalist was *Breakaway* by Cecelia Frey.)

By the following winter, I was back on the family farm. Whenever the mail included a fat letter from my Macmillan editor, Ramsay Derry, I would sit importantly at the Arborite table in the kitchen and "do my revisions." All through that winter, my compelling wish was to leave and go to Edmonton, where I imagined I could join in literary society. My father was reluctantly confronting retirement, and, if I left, it would force his hand. We had far more cattle than he could calve out on his own. For a long time, he and I talked in circles about it, hoping the other would cave in. It was hard for him, and not easy for me, but, to his everlasting credit, the day my father listed our cows for sale, he came home whistling, happy for the first time in a month.

There was a generational mirror image in this, for I believe my father's father had set him free from their farm near the beginning of the Depression. Instead of staying home to scratch a living with his parents, my father was turned loose, to ride the rods and take day work in coal mines in the Crow's Nest Pass and elsewhere. He always spoke of that time with joy on his face: his exciting youth.

Living in a cheap apartment building in Edmonton in the last months of the winter of '73–4 was my next adventure. I was not part of a literary society, not because there wasn't one, but because I didn't know how to find it or enter into it. I was a casual labourer, unloading baler twine from boxcars at a shipping/receiving warehouse.

On an auspicious day, I was invited to the Macdonald Hotel to meet publishing legend Hugh Kane and to see my book's dust jacket for the first time. Hugh offered me a choice of scotch or gin, and asked me questions with generous interest before finally revealing the cover. It was grey, the colour and texture of the asbestos they root out of old attics. The image was of a tortured-looking young male, slightly cross-eyed, with a fratty haircut. I endeavoured not to look sick. Finally, Hugh said, "Ugly, isn't it?" He said he thought it looked like the little silhouette man on Arrow shirts.

When I asked why that was, why my cover was so ugly, he explained that it was very difficult to get artists to read the books for which they were designing and illustrating covers. Hugh had explained Tyrone, my lonesome hero, to the artist at some length, and the first result had been a John Wayne-ish brute. He explained again and got the Arrow shirt man. By then, time was up. Welcome to the world of publishing.

After an eternity of waiting, the pub date arrived. It's the only pub date in thirteen books that I remember: October 4, 1974. Because the novelist competition was a national first, we got a lot of press in the coming month. Jan Truss, Cecelia Frey, and I went the rounds of radio and television stations, and it was enormously exciting for me. The novel was also reviewed across Canada, and I in my innocence believed that was a normal state of affairs. In fact, it would not happen to me again until my novel *The Trade* was nominated for the Giller Prize in 2000.

Because of my youth, twenty-two, my novel and I were novelties. I got a good deal of attention and basked in all of it. Except for the increasingly bad-smelling second novel manuscript that was accumulating on my desk, I felt certain that I was destined for great things.

From three decades of distance, I look back at the young fellow I was in 1974, and I am not embarrassed by him. I'm glad he lived up his brief celebrity. I'm glad he traded on it, however seldom successfully, to meet women. If I have a criticism of him it is only that he suffered a little too theatrically over the inevitable seasons of failure that followed, as he tried desperately to learn how to do what he had already done.

As for *Lonesome Hero*, I like its playfulness. So often the early '70s are depicted as a time of painful earnestness: women in peasant dresses making macramé wall hangings; men in Moroccan shirts smoking hashish off cigarette ends; everybody trooping downtown to protest the war; eastern religions; endless sticks of incense and cups of tea. All that is true enough of the time, except for how it leaves out the irony, the fact that we often understood perfectly how cartoonish we were. There was another reality of the early '70s that was about avoiding work at all costs and trying to live amusingly during all one's waking hours: about how weirdly far we would go to accomplish that. I'm pleased that *Lonesome Hero* is about that funny life and the avoidance of adulthood and its tiresome concerns.

My thanks to Lee Shedden at Brindle and Glass for being interested in giving *Lonesome Hero* another life. It looks as though the interval between the novel's two lives will be almost exactly thirty years.

Fred Stenson
Calgary, October 1, 2004

BEFORE

AFTER

FRED STENSON is the author of thirteen books, including four novels (*Lonesome Hero*, *Last One Home*, *The Trade*, and *Lightning*), two short story collections (*Working Without a Laugh Track* and *Teeth*), and a guide to writing fiction (*Thing Feigned or Imagined*). He is the recipient of the George Bugnet Novel Award, the City of Edmonton Book Prize and a Giller Prize nomination for *The Trade*, two AMPIA Awards for best documentary script, and the Canadian Authors Association Silver Medal for *Lonesome Hero.* He is the only two-time winner of the $25,000 Grant MacEwan Author's Prize. He lives in Calgary with his wife, the author and professor Pamela Banting. He has two children: Ted and Kate.